HOLIDAY CHEESE AND CAPERS

A COZY ROMANTIC HOLIDAY FANTASY

PRIMROSE TALES

CIARA BLUME

DOLCE VILLA PRESS

Published by Dolce Villa Press

www.ciarablume.com

You can't make everybody happy. You're not cheese.

- Anonymous

CONTENTS

ALL A (CHEESE) BOARD

The December air in Geneva held a crisp, crystalline bite that made Minerva Lathrop pull her midnight blue wool traveling cloak tighter as she and Zephyr Nightshade navigated the crowded holiday market alongside the port. The elderly witch still had a spring in her step, despite her one hundred and nine years. She dodged the Ordinary tourists bustling past, laden with shopping bags and fancy digital cameras. They snapped away, dutifully taking photos of every last bauble and garland, but never quite seeing the whole picture, Minerva thought.

The Ordinary folk were entirely unaware of the shimmer in the air just beyond the main dock. To be fair, the cruise line had conjured up a glamor so subtle that even most magical folk might miss it if they weren't looking for it.

"There it is!" Zephyr said, pointing with his free hand while balancing both their suitcases in the other. Despite being one hundred and twelve years old, he insisted on wrangling all their luggage by himself. Minerva knew better than to

"

argue with him. She also knew he'd enchanted the cases to weigh considerably less than they appeared. "It's right over there, just past that bollard with the unusual rust patterns."

"That's not rust, dear, those are runes," Minerva said, squinting at the weathered post. Her still-sharp eyes could read the delicate, magical script even from this distance. The 'Mysteriously Missing from any Maps' Berth Number 7."

Zephyr chuckled, his eyes twinkling with that mischievous spark she'd fallen in love with as a girl, lost for decades, and found again just this past year. "Well, we've never needed a map to find our way into an adventure, have we, Minnie?"

They approached the glamored barrier, a false facade of metal grillwork, and confidently slipped right through to the other side. Minerva felt the familiar tingle of passing through a magical threshold. The world shifted. Not dramatically, but there was a homecoming of sorts whenever she crossed back into the magical world from the Ordinary one. It reminded her of stepping from a noisy room into a hushed library. Now they stood on a private dock that definitely hadn't been visible from the market moments before, and there, floating at least sixteen inches above the water, was *The Celestine Queen,* their home for the next two weeks.

"Oh my!" Minerva breathed, taking in the sight of the luminous cruise ship.

The river cruise ship glowed invitingly in the winter afternoon light. Its outer railings were swathed with evergreen garlands and tiny twinkling lights. Wreaths adorned every polished porthole. A towering Yule tree rose to the apex of the central atrium, its branches heavy with ornaments and shiny silver and gold balls that reflected scenes of merriment inside. Despite being December, the air all around the ship was warmer, touched with holiday enchantment and the promise of adventure.

"Rather spectacular vessel, isn't she?" Zephyr said, slipping his arm through hers. "I'm so glad Bayard sent the invitation for us to join him. It was so thoughtful of him to include us on his inaugural trip with the cruise line, wasn't it?"

"Well... he did say he was inspired to choose a cheese theme for his lecture series because of us!" Minerva reminded Zephyr. "It's kind of like sending a copy of the book to the person you've dedicated it to. Was Bayard always fond of cheese?"

"Cheese, wine, rare flora and fauna, stamps, ciphers..." Zephyr mused. "Our Bayard has always been a bit of a polymath. He picks up new hobbies and passions like some folk pick up new pairs of shoes. Served him well as an information specialist in the The Society for the Protection of Natural Magic and I imagine the Celestine Cruise Line is quite lucky to have him as a guest lecturer now that he's decided to retire. Seems like a perfect gig for him."

"Yes, indeed..." Minerva's voice trailed off and she bit her lip. In all her years, she'd never missed the holidays at home in Primrose Court. It was so strange to be traveling, and she was nervous about spending the holidays amongst strangers. What if Zephyr's old colleague from The Society didn't like her? And what of her customers back home at the fromagerie?

Zephyr patted Minerva's arm. "Come, now. Don't fret about the folks back home, Minnie. The Squeaky Wheel will manage just fine without us for a fortnight. And I know you will get on well with Bayard. He's going to be quite fond of you as well, I predict."

"Mmm." Minerva squeezed his hand. "I do feel a bit guilty, missing Yule in Primrose Court," she admitted. "First holiday season with the fromagerie properly established, and here we are, gallivanting off to Europe. What if I'm needed to help out at the Mudpuddle Bookshop and Cafe?"

"Gallivanting is precisely what people our age should be doing more of," Zephyr declared. "Besides, Maida is perfectly capable of managing the Mudpuddle without you. She's been doing splendidly all year."

"True." Minerva allowed herself a small smile. Handing over the bookshop and café to her great-niece Maida had been easier than she'd expected. It had freed her to pursue a new venture with Zephyr. Who would have thought she'd still be discovering new things about herself at such a ripe old age? It was just a year since she'd learned she was a mouse shifter. That revelation had certainly explained her lifelong obsession with cheese.

"Our staff at the Squeaky Wheel know the holiday inventory backward and forward," Zephyr continued, warming to his theme as they walked toward the gangplank. "We've earned this adventure, Minnie. Time to start making our own traditions, just the two of us. Perhaps we should start a whimsical collection of some sort. Spoons, or holiday ornaments?"

"Cheese forks, obviously." She reached up to brush a biscuit crumb from his silver beard—honestly, the man could eat a single digestive and somehow get crumbs everywhere. "Though I notice you're already making a tradition of collecting crumbs in that beard of yours."

"I'm looking forward to some alone time with you too, my dear," he said with a roguish wink. "You know there are still a few sparks in the fireplace."

"So I've heard..." Minerva laughed, and together they climbed the gangplank toward the glowing ship and whatever delicious mysteries awaited them aboard.

THE ATRIUM of *The Celestine Queen* was a vision of organized chaos. Passengers milled about with champagne flutes, chatting excitedly and admiring the Yule decorations. Everyone stopped to admire the tiered display of cheese samples arranged like a golden pyramid. At the center of it all stood a greeting table draped in forest-green cloth, behind which sat a slight, wire-haired wizard with thick, bushy brows. Beside him sat the most adorable duck Minerva had ever seen.

"Bayard!" Zephyr's face lit up with genuine delight as they approached.

The wizard looked up from his papers, and his eyebrows—practically a life form unto themselves—rose in pleased surprise. "Zeph! You're here! You made it!" He stood, leaning on an elegant walking stick carved with water motifs, and Zephyr quickly rounded the table to embrace him.

Minerva watched the reunion with a warm heart. Zephyr's old friend was smaller than she'd expected, delicately built with a cloudlike fluff of white hair that stood out in all directions. He looked like a benevolent mad scientist. He wore a beautifully cut tweed jacket over a crisp pinstriped shirt, but what caught Minerva's eye were his feet. He had on a pair of bright blue trainers with silver accents that looked decidedly modern and sporty. A colorful paracord bracelet circled one wrist. The effect was charmingly incongruous. Vintage and modern. The distinguished professor meets the adventure sports enthusiast.

"And this must be the famous Minerva," Bayard said, his voice warm as he extended his hand to her. "I'm so pleased to meet the witch who captured this old rogue's heart. You know he used to tell us stories about you, even back in the day."

"Did he, then?" Minerva turned to see Zephyr turning crimson, then she pivoted back to Bayard who was beaming at them. Zephyr was right, she liked this man on sight. There was just something so sincere about him. "The pleasure is all mine," Minerva said, shaking his hand firmly. "Zephyr speaks very highly of you as well. I understand you two got into quite a bit of trouble together."

"Oh, I stayed safely behind while Zeph and Exandra got into all the trouble," Bayard said with a modest smile. "I was the one who had to figure out how to get them out of it."

"Where is Exandra?" Zephyr asked, looking all around. "I thought you said you'd invited her to join us?"

"I did," Bayard sighed, "but of course she was too busy to get away. 'Work comes first!' You know how she is."

"I do." Zephyr shook his head. "But at our age, and at the holidays... I'd just hoped she'd have a change of heart."

"She'd need more than that to take two weeks off from her work with The Society, I'm afraid." Bayard sighed and Minerva noted the wistful, faraway look in his eyes.

"I must admit, I'm disappointed not to get to meet her," Minerva said gently. "I was looking forward to seeing what Zippy calls 'the old gang' back together again."

"*Quack*," the duck added sympathetically, as if in agreement.

"Ah! I almost forgot to introduce you to my familiar!" Bayard exclaimed. "This is Fred." He gestured to his companion. "He's also my research assistant, closest confidant, and occasional voice of reason. He's a Call Duck."

Fred, a perfectly groomed petite duck with pristine white feathers and bright orange feet, gave Minerva an appraising look, then nodded at her as if she'd passed some test.

"He's magnificent," Minerva said sincerely.

"Uh... Mr. Fontaine? Sorry to interrupt but I think these sign-up sheets are supposed to be alphabetical, but someone organized them by cabin number instead, and now I can't find the Andersons, and also should the cheese samples be refrigerated? They're looking a bit warm, and—oh!"

A young man with tousled brown hair and an abundance of nervous energy had appeared at Bayard's elbow, clutching a clipboard and looking thoroughly overwhelmed. He couldn't have been more than twenty-five, with the eager-puppy dog quality of someone desperate to be helpful but unsure how.

"Jasper, don't forget to breathe," Bayard said kindly. "The Andersons are in cabin B-7, the sheets are fine as they are, and the cheese is meant to be served at room temperature."

"Right. Yes. Of course. Room temperature. For the... the flavor profiles." Jasper pushed his glasses up his nose. "I knew that. I definitely knew that."

"Jasper is studying Magical Hospitality in Edinburgh," Bayard explained to Zephyr and Minerva. "He's been invaluable in helping me prepare for this lecture series. He's also working as an intern here on the ship during his school break."

"Is this your first cruise, then?" Zephyr asked the young man.

"First cruise, first real hospitality job, first time working with a celebrity guest lecturer," Jasper said, his words tumbling out. "Not that you're a celebrity, Mr. Fontaine—I mean, you are! In polymath circles. Which are the best circles. The most important circles, when you think about—"

"Excuse me?" a clear, professional voice interrupted. "I'm Wren Connelly, travel blogger for *Enchanted Journeys*. I was hoping to meet Bayard Fontaine? I'm working on an article about the Magical Cheese and Waterways tour."

Minerva turned to see a striking young woman in her mid-twenties, long, auburn hair in a practical braid. She carried a small, lightweight leather satchel and a notebook. She had the crisp, efficient air of someone who took her work seriously.

Jasper's mouth fell open. His clipboard tilted to a dangerous angle and the pen rolled right off it. He lunged to retrieve it before it rolled away.

"Yes! Right! You're on the list!" he said breathlessly, a little too loudly. "Wren Connelly. Travel blogger. VIP. *Very important.* We're so honored. Not that other guests aren't important! Everyone's important. But reviewing us is… you're reviewing us. The tour. With words. That people read."

Wren's lips twitched with amusement. "That is generally how reviews work, yes."

"I'll just—let me find your—" Jasper frantically shuffled papers, dropping several. "Your cabin assignment is—Fred, could you not—"

The duck had waddled over to Wren and was now sitting on her foot, looking up at her with adoring eyes.

"*Quack,*" Fred said admiringly. For such a limited vocabulary, the small duck was remarkably expressive.

"Well, hello there, handsome," Wren said, her professional demeanor softening as she crouched down. "Aren't you a charmer?"

Fred preened, fluffing his feathers.

"Oh, my. He really likes you," Bayard observed. "And Fred is an excellent judge of character."

"I'm a sucker for familiars," Wren admitted, gently stroking Fred's head. "I have a cat at home—just an ordinary one, though. He hates traveling, unfortunately. I miss him already."

"CABIN B-14!" Jasper announced triumphantly, holding up a paper like he'd discovered gold. "You're in cabin B-14. Which is a very good cabin. Probably. I mean, they're all good cabins. But yours is... it has a window."

"Most cabins do," Wren said gently and stood up. Fred promptly sat back down on her foot, in a bid for her attention.

Bayard caught Minerva's eye, and she could see him trying not to laugh.

"Jasper," Bayard said kindly, "why don't you take Fred for a little walk around the deck? I think he needs to stretch his legs before the welcome reception. His harness is in my bag." Bayard pointed to a leather backpack beneath the table.

"Oh. Yes. Of course." Jasper looked relieved to have a concrete task. "Come on, Fred. Let's... stretch... our legs."

Fred gave Wren one last look of longing before waddling after Jasper, who was already muttering to himself again about cheese profiles and cabin assignments.

"That poor boy," Minerva said quietly once Wren had gone. "He seemed quite smitten with the blogger."

"Instant attraction. It happens," Zephyr said with a knowing smile. "Remember when we were that awkward, Min?" Zephyr swiped a pair of champagne glasses from a passing tray and handed one to Minerva.

"Speak for yourself. I was always perfectly composed."

"You once stammered for five full minutes trying to ask me to the Harvest Dance."

"I did no such thing."

"You absolutely did. It was adorable."

Bayard chuckled, making a note on his list. "Well, my intern has a great deal of work to do and Miss Connelly has an article to write. I don't know that there'll be any time for romance, what with all the educational content we have planned."

Zephyr looked stricken. "No time for romance? What kind of nonsense is that, Bayard? This trip is meant to be our honeymoon."

Bayard glanced back at the two of them, a sheepish look coming across his face. "Of course. How silly of me. I mean I planned this whole itinerary as a sort of homage to the two of you."

"Don't you mean a *fromage*?" Zephyr quipped. He wagged his eyebrows for added comic effect.

Minerva groaned. "Zippy, enough with the terrible dad jokes!" Minerva turned to the other man. "I'm sorry, Bayard. Ever since he learned about this particular brand of Ordinary humor, he's been insufferable."

"Very punny." Bayard nodded. "But you knew what I meant. You two have so much to celebrate. You're an inspiration. I wanted this first cruise of my new retirement life to include my old friends."

"I'll drink to that." Zephyr said. He and Minerva raised their glasses and clinked them with Bayard. There was still a hint of sadness around Bayard's eyes, though. He kept scanning the horizon as if looking for someone else, someone missing.

"Now, do you two want to get settled in your cabin before the reception?" Bayard asked. "We'll be serving samples of tomorrow's featured cheese—a beautiful Gruyère de Comté that's essential for proper Yule fondue."

"Point us in the right direction to get to our staterooms," Zephyr said. "Though I reserve the right to sample some of the cheeses while we unpack." Zephyr swiped a few samples from the tiered table to take with them back to their room.

"I would expect nothing less," Bayard said warmly.

As they collected a few flyers with information about the itinerary and headed toward the cabins, Minerva glanced back at the outside deck. Jasper was leaning against the railing, Fred at his feet, watching Wren as she photographed the Yule decorations. She took her notebook out and made a few notes. Even from a distance, through a fogged up window, Minerva could read the young man's expression. Lovestruck. It was a direct hit. Cupid's arrow had pierced the armor of his clipboard.

She smiled to herself. A pinch of romance was always a welcome spice in her book, and particularly around the holidays.

A WHEEL-COME RECEPTION

An hour later, the aft deck lounge was abuzz with excited passengers. A jazz pianist played the classics in one corner and an open bar served signature cocktails in another. Small bar height tables draped in cream linen dotted the area, each topped with a flickering lantern that cast dancing shadows. Servers circulated with trays of champagne that sparkled with tiny star-shaped bubbles. The tiered cheese display was recreated on the light buffet, each level now holding artfully arranged wedges of a pale, almost translucent, ivory-colored cheese.

Minerva and Zephyr had claimed a table near the windows where they could watch the sun make its descent over Geneva's skyline. The Ordinary world felt far away now, separated by more than just the glamor. They were also in that liminal space between land and journey, ready to slip away into adventure.

"Ladies and gentlemen, welcome aboard *The Celestine Queen!*" Bayard stood at a small podium, Fred sat perched on a cushioned stool beside him. The wizard had changed into a more formal tweed jacket, this one with subtle bronze threading that caught the lantern light. His blue trainers, however, remained. "My name is Bayard Fontaine, and I have the tremendous honor of being your guest lecturer for this Yuletide journey through the magical cheese-making regions of Europe."

A small round of applause rippled through the assembled passengers. Minerva counted perhaps forty guests—an intimate group, just as she'd hoped.

"For those who don't know me," Bayard continued, "I spent nearly a century with the French Canadian division of The Society for the Protection of Natural Magic. I mainly worked in the research wing as an information specialist. My true passion as a supernatural anthropologist has always been cultural preservation, including the ways that magic enhances and protects traditional methods of food production, celebration, and consumption. Cheese is a perfect example, and, given the season, seemed like the perfect place to start a lecture series." He paused now, smiling and nodding at Zephyr and Minerva. "And given the fact that I have some old friends who happen to own a fromagerie on board for this trip, you're all sure to be in good hands. If there's any question I can't answer about cheese, I feel confident that Minerva and Zephyr can!"

Minerva felt Zephyr squeeze her hand. This was his old friend's dream—sharing his knowledge with others, traveling the waterways he'd always loved, pursuing joy instead of chasing danger.

"Tomorrow," Bayard said, his voice warming with enthusiasm, "we'll visit our first fromagerie, a family-run operation in the Swiss Alps that produces Gruyère de Comté in the traditional style. But this isn't just any cheese—it's the very foundation of Yule celebrations across all of magical Europe."

He gestured, and Jasper began distributing small plates, each holding a generous wedge of the pale cheese. The intern seemed somewhat less frantic now. Wren was settled two tables over, notebook open, but Minerva noticed she was actually listening more than she was taking notes.

"Gruyère requires *Lactobacillus helveticus* and *Streptococcus thermophilus*. Those are two bacterial cultures that must be kept in perfect balance," Bayard explained. "The cheese ages for a minimum of five months in caves where the temperature never varies more than a single degree. In magical production, the caves themselves are alive with preservation spells, some of which have been maintained for centuries."

Minerva lifted her sample to her nose. The aroma was complex. It smelled nutty, slightly sweet, and had an earthy undertone that could only be attributed to the caves and time.

"This particular wheel is eight months old," Bayard continued. "You'll notice the firm, vaguely granular texture, the way it melts on your tongue. This is what makes proper Yule fondue possible. It must have an even melt, and a depth of flavor and the perfect consistency to hold the kirsch and wine without separating."

Minerva took a bite. Even plain, the cheese was extraordinary. It tasted rich but not overwhelming, with a long, savory finish.

"Magnificent," Zephyr murmured beside her, already reaching for his second piece. "Absolutely magnificent."

"Without this cheese," Bayard said, his voice taking on a more serious note, "hundreds of communities would lose a central part of their Yule celebrations. The tradition of gathering around the fondue pot, the sharing of warmth and sustenance in the darkest time of year, all depends on cheesemakers maintaining their cultures and their craft."

Fred gave a solemn quack as if emphasizing the point for Bayard.

"Over the next fortnight, we'll visit seven fromageries, each producing a cheese essential to Yule traditions. You'll learn about different cultures, aging processes, and the magic that protects these ancient food ways. And, of course, you'll taste some of the finest cheese in the magical world."

More enthusiastic applause. Minerva noticed Wren writing rapidly, a small smile on her face. Jasper, who'd been tasked with refilling champagne flutes, somehow managed to keep drifting toward her table more frequently than the others.

"We depart in thirty minutes," Bayard concluded. "Please enjoy the reception, ask me any questions you might have, and prepare for a journey you won't soon forget."

As the wizard stepped down from the podium, the deck beneath Minerva's feet hummed and vibrated with magic. *The Celestine Queen* was waking up, preparing to fly.

"To adventure," Zephyr said, raising his champagne flute.

"To cheese," Minerva replied, clinking her glass against his.

"To both," he agreed. "And to starting our own traditions, my dear."

She leaned against his shoulder, watching the lights of Geneva begin to twinkle in the gathering dusk. Somewhere below, a crew member called out preparations for departure. The Yule tree's ornaments chimed more urgently, as if excited for the journey.

This was going to be a wonderful trip.

THE SUN HAD DIPPED below the horizon, and the first stars were emerging when a crew member's voice rang out across the deck: "All ashore that's going ashore! The gangplank is rising! All passengers should be aboard!"

Minerva watched with interest as two crew members moved to the boarding ramp, their wands already raised to begin the levitation spell that would retract it. *The Celestine Queen* hummed more insistently beneath her feet, eager to depart.

"WAIT!"

The shout came from the dock below, followed by the thunder of running footsteps.

Every passenger turned to look. Even the servers paused mid-pour.

A figure sprinted toward the gangplank. The dark-skinned woman was impossibly tall, with purple and gray hair streaming behind her like a flag. She wore a trim gray track-suit that somehow managed to look elegant on her imposing frame, and she moved with surprising grace and agility despite her massive size and the heavy-looking pack on her shoulders.

"Hold the plank!" she shouted, her commanding British voice carrying effortlessly across the water.

The crew members exchanged glances, uncertain.

Then came a loud crash from the reception area.

Minerva turned to see Bayard standing frozen at his table, his champagne flute shattered at his feet, stars fizzling out as the golden liquid spread across the deck. His face had gone bright pink beneath his white hair, his bushy eyebrows elevated nearly to his hairline.

Fred, however, had no such paralysis. The duck launched himself from his cushioned stool, flapped to the floor with an excited "*QUACK!*" and waddled out the open door, full speed toward the gangplank, wings still beating.

"Fred, wait!" Bayard started, but his protests went unheeded.

The purple-haired woman leapt onto the gangplank just as the crew began lowering it again. She bounded up the ramp with athletic ease, and the moment she reached the deck, Fred threw himself at her feet, quacking ecstatically and doing a little spinning dance.

"Well, hello, my darling boy," the woman said, and her entire demeanor softened as she crouched down—quite a long way down—to scoop up the handsome duck. Her voice, which had been so commanding and gruff at first, turned gentle and warm. "Did you miss me, Freddy-weddykins? Of course you did! Such a good, sweet boy."

Fred nuzzled into her neck, making contented sounds.

Minerva studied this newcomer with interest. She stood well over six feet tall, with the kind of broad, muscular build that suggested there was giant ancestry somewhere in her bloodline. She was older than she'd seemed at first glance. Perhaps as old as Minerva, even. It was hard to tell with giants. They always seemed ageless. Despite her obvious senior status, there was nothing stooped or frail about her. The giantess inhabited her considerable height with a subtle grace that came from decades of learning to fit herself into a world built too small for her people. Her wavy purple-and-silver streaked hair hung loose, framing a face that was handsome and strong-boned. She had deeply set, ice-blue eyes that missed nothing. And she wasn't shy. She looked up at the crowd of people staring at her, smiled shrewdly, and executed a small bow. She knew her arrival had been a bit melodramatic, and she was prepared to own it.

"Exandra." Zephyr had stood up, and stepped forward toward the newcomer. His voice was somewhere between surprised and delighted. "I thought you were far too busy to come along on a cruise! What in blazes are you doing here?"

"Zephyr Nightshade." She nodded to him with genuine warmth, though she didn't put Fred down. "I might ask you the same thing. Never in a million years would I have expected to see an old agent like you whiling the hours away on a *cruise ship*. A holiday cheese tour, no less!"

"Don't knock it till you've tried it." Zephyr winked, utterly unfazed. "Retirement sure has its perks." He gestured to Minerva. "I'm here with my new bride—"

"Yes, yes. Ms. Lathrop, yes, I'd heard the rumors." Exandra's imperious gaze flicked to Minerva, assessing and dismissing her in the same moment. Her tone remained polite but cool. "You must be the bookshop proprietor."

"Former proprietor," Minerva corrected mildly, refusing to be ruffled. "Current fromagerie owner. And it's Lathrop-Nightshade now."

"You are a mouse shifter as well as a witch, if the rumors are correct?"

"I am," Minerva confirmed. *This giant doesn't beat around the bush*, she thought.

"Interesting. I suppose that explains the cheese obsession." Exandra continued to stare at Minerva, unblinking.

"Amongst other things." Minerva forced herself to keep her chin held high. She'd heard more than a few stories about Zephyr's former partner in fighting magical crimes. She knew the giantess possessed superstrength and a pinch of compulsion. It had made her most valuable when fighting vampires. She was impervious to their wiles. But somehow she wasn't quite what Minerva had pictured. She was... unnerving.

"Exandra." Bayard had finally found his voice. He limped toward them, his cane tapping against the deck. "I... we didn't... ummm...You're not on the passenger manifest." His shoulders slumped. "Your assistant wired me to say you couldn't get away to join us."

"Correct. This is not leisure time for me. I'm here in my official capacity, on a last-minute assignment." She straightened to her full height, still cradling Fred, and suddenly she was all business again. Official, professional, in control. But Minerva noticed the way her fingers twitched as they stroked Fred's feathers. Most suspicious.

"We've received some troubling reports of cheese-related incidents that require further investigation before they escalate."

"Incidents?" Bayard's voice cracked slightly.

"Yes. Some of them at fromageries along this route." Exandra's eyes swept across the assembled passengers, most of whom were still watching her with undisguised curiosity. "Someone's been targeting magical cheese production. Sabotaging cultures, damaging equipment. The Society was only just made aware."

Bayard's face somehow got even paler. "I... I see."

"They're calling the perpetrator the Culture Vulture," Exandra continued. She was looking at everyone except Bayard now, her jaw set. "It all sounds dramatic, I know, but accurate. Someone's threatening Yule cheese production across the region. I'm here to make sure everyone on this tour stays safe and sound and to catch whoever's responsible."

Zephyr frowned. He glanced from Exandra to Bayard. "That sounds very concerning. Bayard, did you know about this?"

"I... I had heard there was a small incident at one of the fromageries upstream," Bayard admitted, still staring at

Exandra. "Nothing major, though. I didn't think it was a big deal."

"Well, it's considered to be a major big deal now." Exandra looked directly at him, and for just a brief moment, something raw, vulnerable, and protective flashed across her face. Then her professional mask slid back into place. "So I'm afraid you'll be stuck with me keeping you all safe for the duration of the cruise."

"That's... that's fine, absolutely fine!" Bayard managed. "Of course. We're happy to cooperate with the investigation. Aren't we, Fred?"

Fred, still in Exandra's arms, quacked his agreement while simultaneously trying to worm his way into the pouch pocket of her track suit.

"I should find the captain to brief him and get myself settled," Exandra said abruptly. "Sorry for the dramatic entrance, Bay. Didn't mean to crash your party."

She set Fred down with obvious reluctance, and the duck immediately positioned himself between her and Bayard, looking up at both of them as if existentially torn between which one he wanted to follow. His obvious confusion was almost heartbreaking. Bayard scooped him up and patted him, murmuring words of comfort.

As Exandra strode away toward the ship's interior, her pack over one shoulder, Minerva noticed the tiniest hitch in her confident stride. It was just for a moment after she walked out the door, a flash of hesitation that looked like something else.

Bayard stood rooted to the spot, watching her go.

"Well," Zephyr said. "I for one am delighted to have the old gang all back together. I'm sure whatever the Culture Vulture has in store, they're no match for a crack agent like our Exxie."

LATER THAT EVENING, after the reception dispersed, a smaller group gathered near the bow for the sail away. Bayard, Zephyr, Minerva, Wren (notebook ever present), and Jasper, who'd been tasked with fetching a tray of after-dinner cordials, tossed magical, eco-safe confetti over the railing. It glided down toward the river in shimmering ribbons before evaporating.

Exandra stood a few feet apart from the group. She was leaning against the railing with her back to the receding lights of Geneva, watching them.

Before long, the ship had begun its journey, floating smoothly above the darkening water. The hum of magic beneath their feet had settled into a pleasant, rhythmic thrum.

"So, Exandra," Zephyr said, accepting a small glass of something amber from Jasper's tray. "Tell us about these incidents you mentioned."

Exandra stroked Fred's feathers, her expression carefully neutral. "Three fromageries have been hit in the past month. Different regions, different cheese styles, but the perp has had the same pattern every time. Either the cultures are compromised or the aging processes are disrupted. Nothing catastrophic, but it might be enough to threaten Yule cheese production. The Culture Vulture seems to have it in for the holidays."

"Can you say anything more about this? What kind of compromises are we talking about?" Wren asked, pen poised expectantly over her notebook. Her journalist instincts were clearly engaged. "How odd that we haven't heard anything about this in the mainstream magical news!"

"That's not surprising." Zephyr tutted. "You'd be shocked at the things that go unreported on a daily basis. We agents rarely speak to the press during an active investigation. Too dangerous. It compromises us and the case."

Exandra shrugged and nodded. But she turned to Wren with a look of respect.

"What can I say without getting too specific..." Her voice was professional, detached, but not unkind. "I can say it's always something that could be explained as an accident or negligence. But the timing is too coincidental, we think. Someone knows exactly what they're doing."

Bayard had gone very quiet, his fingers white-knuckled on his walking stick. "And you think... this tour might be targeted?"

"The fromagerie we're visiting tomorrow was on a list of potential targets." Exandra turned to look at him directly, and Minerva saw something flicker between them again. Concern, tension, or was it something else entirely? "I couldn't risk anything happening to—I mean, I thought it best to be here. Just in case."

"Quite right. I would have made the same call," Zephyr said firmly. "Though I'm surprised the Society sent you alone. No partner on this mission? Isn't that highly irregular?"

A muscle tightened in Exandra's jaw. "Everyone else was either off for the holiday or already away on assignment. Or *retired*." She spat out the "r" word like it left a terrible taste in her mouth. "There was nobody else. I had to come alone."

"What a hardship for you that must be..." Bayard murmured, so quietly Minerva almost missed it.

"This is fascinating," Wren said, writing rapidly. "I mean—not fascinating that someone's sabotaging cheese production. That's terrible. But from a story perspective..." She grinned apologetically.

"Perhaps we should try to keep this quiet?" Jasper interrupted nervously. "I mean, we don't want to alarm the passengers. Or get bad press before Mr. Fontaine's lecture series even properly starts."

He shot an apologetic glance at Wren, who raised an eyebrow.

"I'm a journalist, not a gossip columnist," she said coolly. "I know the difference between a story and fearmongering."

"Right. Yes. Of course you do. I just meant—" Jasper's ears turned red. "Sorry."

"The boy's right," Exandra barked out, and Minerva noticed Jasper straighten slightly at being called "right" by someone so imposing. "No need to alarm everyone. I'll investigate discreetly. Most passengers won't even know I'm working."

"I think it's a little late for that," Minerva commented. "Given your dramatic arrival. The other passengers are not simpletons. They already know something's up."

"And what if something happens at tomorrow's fromagerie?" Bayard asked. His voice was steady, but Minerva could see the tension in his shoulders.

"Then I'll handle it." Exandra's tone brooked no argument. "That's what I do, Bayard. It's what we've always done and what I intend to keep doing, with or without you."

The words hung in the air between them, weighted with history Minerva didn't fully understand. Zephyr clearly did, though. His expression had grown wary as his gaze moved between his two old colleagues.

Fred quacked softly, and Exandra looked down at him. "Don't worry, darling. I definitely won't let anything happen to you. You are one of my top priorities. I even noted it in my brief. 'Must protect Fred.'"

The gentleness in her voice when she spoke to the duck was so at odds with her professional demeanor that it made Minerva's heart ache a little.

"Well," Zephyr said, breaking the tension, "I for one am glad you're here, Exandra. It'll be like old times. The three of us on an adventure together."

"If you can call it that," Exandra said, but something in her expression softened. "Not much of an adventure, really, when we're just babysitting some cheese cultures."

"I don't know, that sounds like the best kind of adventure to me," Minerva chimed in. When Exandra's cool gaze turned to her, she met it evenly. "I've found that the most interesting things happen when you're paying attention to the small, important details, Agent Thorne. Cheese cultures. Bakery recipes. All those little traditions that hold communities together."

For a moment, something like understanding flickered in Exandra's eyes. Then she nodded curtly. "Quite."

Suddenly a melodious, magical chime that seemed to come from everywhere and nowhere sounded through the ship's PA system.

"That's the signal for evening turndown service," Jasper said. "We should head to our cabins. We'll fly through the night and arrive at the Alpine fromagerie by morning."

"So we're actually going to be flying, not sailing?" Wren asked, looking intrigued.

"Yes, we'll be taking to the air for a good part of the journey. The ship hops between waterways," Bayard explained, some of his natural enthusiasm returning. "We'll lift higher now and travel overland till tomorrow. You'll see the Alps by moonlight if you look out your porthole before you go to sleep. It's quite spectacular."

"I should document that," Wren said, already making notes.

"I could... show you the best viewing spot?" Jasper offered hesitantly. "For the Alps. If you want. For your article."

Wren glanced up, and her expression softened a bit. "That would be helpful. Thank you, Jasper."

The young man looked like he might faint from happiness.

As the group began to disperse toward their cabins, Minerva lingered at the railing with Zephyr. Ahead of them, Bayard limped toward the interior, Fred tucked under his arm.

Exandra had already disappeared into the ship's depths.

"There's a story there with those two, isn't there?" Minerva commented.

"Several stories," Zephyr agreed. "And I suspect that it's still being written. Should be an interesting chapter!" He wagged his eyebrows.

The ship rose higher, and the lights of Geneva fell away below them. Above, the stars blazed in the winter sky. Ahead, somewhere in the darkness, the Alps waited.

FROMAGE THE BEGINNING

Morning light painted the Swiss Alps in shades of rose and gold as *The Celestine Queen* settled down onto a small, frozen mountain lake, its hull barely kissing the ice. Minerva stood at the railing with her coat buttoned against the crisp air, watching drifts of snow blow across the lake's surface like ghostly dancers.

"Fromagerie Sommet is somewhere up there." Zephyr pointed toward a cluster of buildings nestled into the mountainside. "Bayard says it's been in the same family for seven generations."

"How will we get up there?" Minerva asked.

"Acutally, I think I hear our ride arriving now." Zephyr held a hand to his ear. Minerva heard the hoofbeats, too. Three wooden wagons, painted with simple floral motifs, were headed their way, pulled by large, handsome brown horses with bells on their padded harnesses. One of the drivers waved as they pulled the wagons up alongside the banks of the lake.

"I'd better bring a sweater." Minerva reached for her favorite cardigan, a soft blue cashmere wool with mother of pearl buttons and secret pockets. The embroidered acorns around the collar always reminded her of the literary squirrels back home in Primrose Court. She wondered what they were reading in their book club this week.

FIFTEEN MINUTES LATER, they piled into the waiting wagons, lined with warm blankets and with complimentary thermoses full of hot mulled cider to be enjoyed on the short trip up the mountainside. Minerva noticed Exandra emerging last from the cruise ship. Her hair was coiled efficiently at the nape of her neck beneath a close-fitting knit beanie cap. She wore practical hiking boots, thick leggings, and a black, high-tech down parka with the Society logo on the back. She cut an impressive figure. The mountains reflected off her mirrored aviator sunglasses as she scanned the perimeter, assessing the risks and cataloguing the terrain.

Bayard saw her, too. They nodded at each other and then he quickly looked away, his grip tightening on his walking stick as he climbed into the sled with Minerva and Zephyr.

The mountainside Swiss town looked like something from a storybook, with traditional Alpine architecture, carved wooden balconies, and flower boxes that would be overflowing with geraniums in the summertime. But as they drew closer, Minerva noticed more modern touches: solar panels disguised as roof tiles, gleaming mechanized windows that probably had magical climate controls, and outside the fromagerie, what looked like a brand-new loading dock.

Bayard sat at the front of the wagon, Fred's carrier in his lap, pointing out features to the assembled passengers. "The Sommet family has been making Gruyère since 1847, but the current generation has introduced some welcome innovations while still maintaining the traditional methods that make their cheese exceptional."

Jasper sat beside Wren, a notebook full of facts balanced on his knee. "Did you know that authentic Gruyère can only be made in certain regions of Switzerland? It's a protected designation of origin, which means—"

"I did know that, actually," Wren said gently, her camera already out and capturing the golden morning light on the mountains. "But thank you."

Jasper's face fell.

"But did you know that Gruyère cheese is high in calcium, K2, vitamin B12, and essential Omega fatty oils?" Jasper ticked off some of the health benefits of the cheese. "It's good for heart health, skin health, nerve health…"

"Plus it tastes delicious." Bayard patted Jasper's arm in a hopeful bid to slow down his blathering prattle. "I think that's what most of us will be focused on today."

"It's impressive that you've researched so thoroughly." Wren smiled, glancing at him. "Most hospitality students wouldn't have bothered."

His expression brightened. "Really? I just wanted to make sure I could answer questions if anyone asked. Not that you would need to ask me. You probably know so much more than I do. You don't need me to—"

"Jasper." She smiled. "Breathe."

He took a visible breath, then laughed at himself. "Right. Breathing. I can do that."

Zephyr caught Minerva's eye and they shared a knowing look. Crushes were so delightfully awkward.

As soon as the cruisers climbed out from the wagons, they were greeted by a young couple. The man was tall and broad-shouldered with clear skin, rosy cheeks, and an easy smile. The woman beside him had her blonde hair pulled back in a practical bun and wore an apron over sturdy work clothes.

"Welcome, welcome!" the man called out. His English was excellent, with only the faintest trace of an accent. "I am Lukas Sommet, and this is my wife, Anja. We are so honored to host you as one of your stops on the Celestine Line's cheese tour."

"The honor is ours," Bayard said warmly, shaking their hands. "Your reputation precedes you. I've heard wonderful things about your recent modernization efforts."

Anja beamed. "We've worked very hard. My grandfather was set in the old ways, you know. He steadfastly refused to make any changes to the way we do things. I understand... what is that saying?" Anja's accent was a bit thicker than Lukas's., "Don't fix what isn't broke?" She smiled wistfully, obviously thinking of her grandpère. "Still, when he passed and left us the fromagerie, Lukas and I knew we wanted to honor tradition while also embracing what magic and technology could offer."

"A delicate balance," Zephyr observed.

"Very delicate," Lukas agreed. "But worth it. Come, let me show you all what we've accomplished."

THE ENTRANCE to the fromagerie opened into a modern visitor center—gleaming counters, interactive displays about cheese-making, and a small café area where guests could sample products. But just beyond, through large windows, they could see the heart of the operation: the production room with its massive copper vats and bustling workers.

"First, let me show you our control room," Lukas said with obvious pride. "This is where we monitor everything, temperature, humidity, bacterial cultures. All magical, all precise."

He opened a door off the main corridor to reveal a small chamber filled with glowing instruments and interactive wall charts that updated in real-time. Minerva glimpsed rows of numbers, graphs showing temperature curves, and what looked like a map of the extensive cave system beneath the building.

"Quite impressive," Bayard murmured. "The network of caves looks like it goes on forever."

"Indeed," Exandra agreed. She stroked her chin thoughtfully. "So many places to hide."

Minerva saw her taking mental notes.

"But come away from all this," Anja said, already moving ahead. "The real magic happens in the production room. This way, everybody!"

THE PRODUCTION ROOM smelled strongly of warm milk and sharp, clean copper. Three enormous vats dominated the space, each large enough to hold at least a thousand gallons. Workers moved with practiced efficiency, stirring, testing, monitoring.

"Gruyère begins with pure, raw cow's milk," Bayard explained to the group, falling naturally into his professorial voice. The group clustered around him, and Minerva noticed how he came alive when teaching. His slight limp was forgotten as his whole being focused on sharing with the group. "The cheesemakers add the two specific bacterial cultures, *Lactobacillus helveticus* and *Streptococcus thermophilus*, to get the process started. These aren't just ingredients. They're living communities that have been carefully maintained, sometimes for centuries."

"Like sourdough starter?" someone in the group shouted out.

"Exactly like sourdough starter," Bayard confirmed. "And just as temperamental. The cultures must be kept at precise temperatures, fed regularly, and protected from contamination."

Anja stepped forward to personalize the tour. "Our family maintains a culture library in a specialized chamber. My great-grandmother started it in 1923. Every morning, I check on the cultures like I would check on my own children."

Lukas demonstrated the heating process, the careful monitoring as the milk reached exactly thirty-two degrees Celsius. "The timing is everything," he said. "Too hot, and you kill the cultures. Too cold, and they won't activate properly. You must pay attention. Listen to what the cheese is telling you."

They watched as rennet was added, and the milk began to coagulate into curds. Next the workers cut the curds with specialized harps, and stirred them slowly, methodically.

"How long does it all take?" Wren asked, her camera clicking softly as she documented the process.

"From milk to a shaped wheel, about four hours of active production," Bayard said. "Then the wheels are pressed, brined, and moved to the aging caves. That's where time truly does its magic."

Jasper had been listening intently, occasionally glancing at his notecards but mostly watching Wren. When she moved to get a better angle for a photograph, he quickly stepped forward to hold back a hanging cord that might have been in her way.

"Thank you," she said, surprised and a bit delighted when his hand lightly brushed her collarbone.

"I just—I noticed you like to frame people in your shots. Not just the equipment. The workers, their hands, their faces."

She lowered her camera, looking at him with new interest. "You noticed all that?"

"I do some photography, too. For events and food styling. I love capturing the joy in people's expressions when they taste something amazing, or the pride on a chef's face when they plate something beautiful." He flushed. "Sorry, I'm rambling again."

"No," Wren said slowly. "That's extremely insightful. Most people think food photography is just about trying to make the food look good. But it's really about telling the story of how it reached the table, isn't it? The people behind it who made that happen, the ingredients, the time and care..."

"Exactly!" His face lit up. "That's exactly it."

They smiled at each other, and Minerva felt her heart warming. She couldn't help herself. She was hoping the two youngsters would hit it off.

"Now," Lukas said, gesturing for them to follow him, "let's take a peek inside the aging caves. This is where the cheese truly becomes Gruyère."

They descended a stone staircase into cool dimness. The caves were carved into the mountain itself, with rough stone walls and wooden shelving that stretched far back into shadows. As far as one could see, wheels of cheese lined the open shelves like golden coins, each one marked with dates and batch numbers.

"We age our standard Gruyère for five to eighteen months," Anja explained. "But you can't simply count the days and declare it finished. The cheese tells you when it's ready."

"How?" someone asked.

Anja nodded at Bayard, encouraging him to field the question.

"The texture, the aroma, the way it sounds when you tap it," Bayard said. "A properly aged Gruyère has a particular resonance. And the taste—" He closed his eyes briefly. "When it's perfectly aged, there's a moment of absolute harmony. All the flavors in balance. That's when you know it's finished with that stage. It's time for the cheese to come up out of the cave, into the light, and be savored."

Bayard's eyes opened and landed directly on Exandra, who stood at the back of the group. She was looking at him, too. He folded his arms across his chest and raised his eyebrows at her. She mirrored his stance, wrapping her own arms across her body and tilting her head defiantly at him.

They were locked in some kind of personal challenge, an inside joke, having something to do with their past, and nothing to do with the cheese.

Time to be savored, Minerva thought. She reached for Zephyr's hand, and found she didn't have far to grasp as he was already reaching for hers.

"Pardon the interruption." Exandra chose this moment to call out, her voice cutting through the reverent atmosphere.

"But I need to use the facilities. Can you point me in the right direction?"

"Back toward the entrance." Anja waved toward the staircase.

Bayard watched her go, his expression troubled. He'd been afraid to even hope she would come on this trip. And now that she was here, even if it wasn't for the reasons he'd hoped, there was so much he wanted to say to her. But it would have to wait. He turned back to the group with a forced smile. "Okay, cruisers. Shall we continue the tour?"

The tour continued through the caves, Lukas explaining their plans to expand into some of the unused chambers, Anja pointing out plaques commemorating wheels that had won awards, Bayard adding educational tidbits about aging processes and flavor development.

Jasper was consulting his notecards again, trying to walk and read at the same time, when his foot caught on an uneven stone. The cards flew from his hands, scattering across the cave floor like autumn leaves.

"Oh no, I'm so sorry, I—" He dropped to his knees, scrambling to gather them.

Wren pulled out her wand with a small smile. "*Collectus*," she said, and the cards rose from the ground, stacking themselves neatly. She plucked them from the air and slipped them into Jasper's jacket pocket.

"You don't need these to impress me, you know," she said.

Jasper looked up at her from his knees, his face flushing. "I don't?"

"No." She offered him a hand up. "You're doing just fine on your own."

He took her hand, standing slowly, and for a moment they just looked at each other.

"Come on, you two kids," someone called from ahead. "We're almost to the tasting room!"

As they hurried to catch up, Jasper did a terrible job of hiding his enormous smile.

Next, Anja led them past rows of aging wheels to a heavy wooden door with a small window at the center. "This is the special chamber where we age our famous Yule cheese," she said softly, almost reverently. "We keep this one entirely traditional—no magical climate controls, just the natural stability of the deep cave. We monitor it constantly, but we let the mountain itself do the aging work."

Through the window, everyone got a glimpse of dozens of cheese wheels glowing softly in the dim light, each marked with a golden sunburst symbol.

"These will all be ready for Yule Eve," Lukas said. "They're already committed to magical communities across the region. These little wheels of cheese will be the fondue centerpieces on hundreds of magical Yule tables. They will bring so much joy to families near and far. I still remember how we fought as children for the honor of being the first one to dip bread into the Yule fondue crock."

PANIC AT THE CHEESE CO

The rustic tasting room was located even deeper back inside the caves, past the Yule cheese chamber. This was as far from the main entrance as the public was allowed and was a great place to conclude the tour.

The rounded-out space consisted of a cozy room with long wooden tables. A small space heater was running in the corner to combat the cave's natural chill. Red and white checkered cloths covered the tables. Samples of various aged Gruyères stood on wooden boards beside large wooden bowls filled with slices of fresh, crusty bread.

"Now," Bayard said, "this is where you can truly appreciate the differences between—"

A piercing alarm shattered the peaceful atmosphere.

Everyone jumped. Fred, who'd been dozing contentedly in Bayard's backpack, exploded into frantic quacking.

"What's happening?" Anja cried out.

Exandra came rushing back from the direction of the entrance, her face flushed, her expression alarmed. "Someone's broken into the facility! The control room's been ransacked! I think it's the work of the Culture Vulture!"

THE GROUP SURGED BACK toward the entrance, following Exandra's lead. Minerva gripped Zephyr's hand as they hurried through the stone corridors. Something was not quite right. Her mouse-sharp senses tingled with wrongness.

Behind her, Bayard moved surprisingly fast, despite his limp.

"Something's not right, Fred," he mumbled. "It doesn't make any sense."

The control room door hung open. Even from the corridor they could all see the damage. Drawers were pulled out from the desk and papers were scattered across the floor. One of the interactive charts flickered erratically.

"No, no, no," Lukas was saying, pushing past into the room. "Who would do this? Why?"

Anja was already at the main console, her hands flying over the magical controls. "The Yule chamber is offline. The monitoring's been disabled. I can't see the temperature readings."

"It's the Culture Vulture," Exandra said grimly. "This matches the pattern from the other incidents."

But Minerva barely heard her. Something was wrong. She could sense it. Her nose twitched, and she caught a shift in temperature that didn't bode well: warm air, too warm and too much of it, moving where it shouldn't.

"Something's wrong with the temperature in the Yule cheese room," she said, her voice cutting through the panic.

Everyone turned to look at her. Bayard raised a suspicious eyebrow.

"I can sense it," she explained. "And I can smell it. The air flow is wrong. There's hot air…" She closed her eyes, sniffing the air and letting her mouse instincts guide her. "It's flowing into the Yule cheese chamber. Something's heating it up."

"But the door to that chamber is sealed," Anja protested. "It's always—"

Minerva was already moving, already shifting into her mouse form as she ran. Her clothes shrank with her as she became a small gray mouse, whiskers twitching, nose pulling her toward the danger. She sensed Zephyr behind her keeping pace and heard multiple footsteps pounding behind them as they raced down the stone corridor.

Sure enough, the door to the Yule chamber stood wide open.

Minerva's mouse heart hammered as she scurried in, immediately feeling the heat blasting in from the tasting chamber next door. Someone had propped both doors open and turned the space heater to maximum. Hot, dry air was flooding into the carefully maintained cave. The thermostat was hanging by its wires, barely still attached to the wall. It had been deliberately disconnected.

She shifted back to human form just as the others arrived.

"The thermostat's been tampered with," Minerva said, pointing. "And the space heater's been used to warm the air deliberately, I think. Look! The doors have been propped."

"The cheese," Anja gasped, moving toward the glowing wheels. "The cultures—if the temperature rose too high—"

"How long has it been?" Zephyr asked sharply, already pulling out his wand.

"Minutes," Lukas said, his voice breaking. "Maybe ten minutes of exposure? The wheels are still cool to the touch, but—"

"We still have time." Zephyr moved to the center of the chamber, his wand glowing. "Minerva, cast with me. Lukas, Anja, reconnect that thermostat. Everyone else, clear the doorway."

Minerva took her position beside Zephyr, feeling their magic align as it always did. It was as natural as breathing, even after all their years apart. The last few precious months together had only strengthened the bond that was always there. She focused on the air itself, feeling its temperature, its movement, while Zephyr drew the excess heat away from the chamber, pulling it up and out through ventilation shafts that suddenly glowed with blue light.

"*Frigus conservare*," they chanted together, their combined magic creating a cooling ward that settled over the precious wheels like a protective blanket.

Anja's hands moved frantically over the reconnected thermostat, adjusting settings, restoring the careful balance. Lukas sealed the doors, shutting out the warm air from the cave.

For several long minutes, the only sounds were the hum of magic, the soft clicking of the restored equipment, and Fred's worried quacking from Bayard's backpack.

After some delay, Anja let out a shaky breath. "The temperature's stabilized. We're back to optimal range."

"The wheels?" Zephyr asked.

Lukas had his hands on one, his eyes closed, listening to something only a master cheesemaker could hear. "They're... they're all right. The cultures survived. We caught it in time."

The relief in the tasting room was palpable. Anja burst into tears, and Lukas pulled her close. Several of the tour passengers were hugging each other. Jasper looked like he might pass out.

"You don't think," Wren asked cautiously, "that this Culture Vulture might still be here, hiding in the caves?"

"Impossible," Exandra said, reappearing in the tasting room again. "That's not their MO. Besides, whoever did this wouldn't risk sticking around for the meltdown. Have you ever smelled that much spoilt cheese?" She grimaced and waved a hand in front of her face, banishing the idea of that smell.

"Thank you," Anja said, wiping her eyes. "Thank you all so much. Without you, all those families, all those traditions we cherish—they would have been ruined."

"We'll send a special crate to your shop," Lukas added. "The Squeaky Wheel, yes? Our finest wheels. It's the least we can do."

Minerva smiled warmly. "That's very kind, but we were happy to help."

"You saved the Yule," Anja insisted. "That deserves more than kind words."

Exandra sat down heavily at one of the tables and helped herself to a wedge of cheese and a hunk of bread. Despite herself, her eyes closed as she chewed. She nearly moaned with pleasure at the taste of the delicious cheese. No wonder people were so crazy about the stuff.

"You okay, Agent?" Zephyr teased.

"I'm fine," Exandra snapped. "Just a little peckish. I skipped breakfast." As she emerged from her momentary reverie, she resumed her normal, impassive expression. Her voice was hardened again when she spoke.

"I'll need to file a complete report. This was a deliberate sabotage, clearly meant to destroy the Yule production. The Culture Vulture is more brazen than we thought."

She glanced toward the alcove where Minerva and Zephyr still stood, and an odd look flashed across her face—frustration? Disappointment? Jealousy? It was gone so quickly, Minerva almost missed it.

"Thanks for handling the problem, Zeph," Exandra said, her voice carefully neutral. "I was just coming back down to—"

"You should thank my bride, not me, don't you think?" Zephyr asked. "Minerva's keen senses detected the problems before any of their fancy equipment did." He placed an arm around Minerva's shoulders. "She's quite remarkable. It's not the first time her wonderful instincts have saved the day."

Exandra's jaw tightened almost imperceptibly. "Yes. Of course. Great work, mouse lady. Very... efficient."

She stood and turned stiffly to head back to the entrance. Bayard watched her go, brow furrowed, his expression a mix of bewilderment and worry. He waited till everyone else left before following her out.

THE TRIP back to *The Celestine Queen* was subdued. Before they climbed into the sleds that were waiting to tender them back to the ship, Lukas and Anja pressed gifts on them—small wheels of their standard Gruyère, and gratitude that bordered on overwhelming.

Wren had photographed everything. She'd captured the control room damage, the rescued cheese wheels, the relief on Anja's face, Minerva and Zephyr standing together after the magical work. Now she sat snuggled in warm blankets in the sled, sipping hot cider and reviewing her shots, occasionally showing one to Jasper, who leaned in close to see the small screen.

"You got some good ones," he said. "This one of the cheese-makers hugging. Goodness! The relief on their faces. You can imagine exactly what they almost lost."

"Thank goodness it turned out okay." Wren scrolled through more images. "I got far more of a story than I expected today. I'm not even sure how I'll write about it."

As EVENING FELL and the ship prepared to depart, Bayard found Exandra standing alone on the deck. She was staring out at the Alps, which were turning purple in the fading light.

"Exandra."

She didn't turn. "I'm writing up my report shortly. But you should know that my initial findings suggest organized sabotage with knowledge of cheesemaking processes. The perpetrator had to know exactly which controls to disable, exactly how to—"

"You don't really think there's a Culture Vulture, do you?" Bayard interrupted, his voice strained. He couldn't believe what she was saying. "I mean, beyond that trouble upstream that I reported to the director. You knew that was me who called it in, right? I thought maybe it was a prankster, someone playing silly games. I never imagined it might be something more..." He gripped his cane tighter.

What had he been thinking when he made up that crazy story?

But he knew the answer. He'd been thinking, no, *hoping*, that if there was some sort of threat, Exandra might want to join them on the tour. He never once imagined that the threat he'd made up might really exist. Careful what you wish for, indeed!

"What do you mean, *do I really think there's a Culture Vulture*?" Exandra narrowed her eyes at him. "What are you suggesting, Bayard Fontaine?"

"Nothing, nothing at all…" Bayard waved a hand in the air. "If it is something after all, I guess I'm glad you're here. Truly. I just hope you're not too inconvenienced. I didn't think they'd send one of their best agents out, especially during the holidays. This must be more serious than I realized."

Exandra's shoulders stiffened. When at last she turned to face him, her eyes were bright. Whether that was with anger or unshed tears, he couldn't tell.

"You *guess you're glad* I'm here?" Her voice was sharp. "You didn't *think* they'd send *me*? What exactly are you trying to say, Bayard?"

"I just meant—" He floundered. "I didn't expect the Society to take it so seriously. To pull you away from—"

"From what?" She stepped closer, and he could see the hurt beneath her defensive anger. "From my very important, very full life? From all the better places I should be spending my holidays?"

"No! That's not—"

"It *is* serious," she said, her voice tight. "And I intend to get to the bottom of it. Whether you think I'm needed here or not."

"Exandra, I didn't mean—"

But she was already walking away, her tall frame rigid with wounded pride, disappearing into the ship's interior.

Bayard stood frozen, replaying the conversation, trying to understand how his gratitude and guilt and relief had come out so terribly wrong. In his carrier, Fred stirred and quacked softly—a sound of sympathy.

"I've totally mucked that up haven't I, Fred?" Bayard whispered.

Fred didn't quack back. He just tucked his head under his wing.

BELOW DECK LATER THAT EVENING, Minerva watched Zephyr standing at their porthole, watching the Alps recede into the distance as the ship rose gracefully into the clear night sky. He was deep in thought, brow furrowed as he stroked his lush silver beard.

"Penny for your thoughts?" she asked.

"I was just thinking about Bayard and Exandra," he said. "This should be a happy time for Bayard. But I don't think Exandra's happy about us all moving on to other things and leaving her behind. Especially Bay. Those two care a lot for each other. Always have. But they've always been completely unable to express their feelings and say what they actually mean. Things have never been quite the same since Bayard had his accident." Zephyr signed. "It happened toward the end of our training. We'd always assumed we'd end up working in the field together. But when Bayard got injured, it radically altered his trajectory, and ours, too. He never returned to the field." Zephyr tugged at his beard thoughtfully. "Who knows what would have blossomed between him and Exandra if they hadn't been split up like that. I just hate seeing them so twisted up and miserable."

"Mmm." Minerva slipped her arm through his. "The unable-to-express-their-feelings part reminds me of two people I used to know. Spent decades circling each other, never quite brave enough to speak the truth…"

He pulled her close. "Thank goodness we eventually figured it out. Now we get to do all the fun stuff together and make up for lost time."

"Thank goodness, indeed." She rested her head on his shoulder. "Though I'm starting to fear that all the excitement on this cruise might pull you out of retirement."

"You're seriously worried about the Culture Vulture?" Zephyr smirked.

"Amongst other things." She thought of Bayard's guilty expression, Exandra's too-perfect discovery of the break-in, the way both of them seemed more confused than truly alarmed. "Something about it doesn't quite add up, Zippy."

"Your mouse nose tingling?"

"Something like that."

"I'm so glad you said so, Minnie." He held her closer and kissed the top of her head. "Something's not adding up for me, either. But one thing I'm sure of. Your instincts are sharp as any Society agent's that I've worked with to date. We'll get to the bottom of this mystery, together."

THE ROQUEFORT RIGAMAROLE

The French countryside unfolded beneath *The Celestine Queen* like a pastoral painting in muted wintry tones. They floated past rolling hills striped with vineyards and stone villages clustered around church spires, and in the distance, Minerva spied the dramatic limestone cliffs that housed some of the world's most storied cheese caves.

As the ship slowly descended toward a private, sheltered landing near the village of Roquefort-sur-Soulzon, Minerva carried her mug of morning tea to the railing. She almost gasped with delight when she first spotted the flock. A small group of sheep grazed on a hillside, their cotton candy-like wool reflecting the morning light in impossible colors. One ewe's coat shimmered with an opalescent blue, another with soft, pale lavender rose, a third glowed bright with hints of the honey gold tones of whipped nougat.

"Ah! You've spied the famous magical sheep," Bayard said, following her gaze. He stood a few feet from her at the railing with his travel journal, making notes. "You should see them in August. Their coats reach peak saturation in late summer."

"Wow! They're still so beautiful now," Wren said, rushing to join them at the railing. Her camera was already in hand but then she lowered it with a frustrated sigh. "Though we're not supposed to take any photos. Ratty bats! I suppose I'll have to enjoy everything with just my eyes today."

"I was just about to mention that." Jasper wasn't far behind. He came over to stand beside her.

Minerva wrinkled her brow. "What's that about?"

"Fromagerie Valmont has a strict no-photography policy on their grounds," Bayard explained. "We were lucky to even get a tour there. I had to pull strings. Philippe Valmont is very protective of his methods and presentation."

"Protective is putting it mildly." Wren nodded. "I read he once tried to sue a journalist for describing the atmosphere in his caves in too much detail. He claimed she violated his NDA by painting too vivid of a picture."

"That reminds me!" Jasper smacked his forehead. "I need to make sure I have all the NDAs gathered from all the guests attending the tour. There's still one or two that I need to collect. Excuse me?" He looked apologetically at Wren, who waved him off with one hand.

"Go!" she said. "Duty calls!" Then she turned back toward Minerva and Bayard. "I'm very excited about today's tour. It's a plum assignment. So few bloggers have been allowed in. Even if I can't take photos, I'm excited to see it."

"I just hope nothing else goes wrong." Minerva sipped her tea, watching Bayard carefully.

He nodded his agreement and then excused himself when they heard the rolling clatter of the anchor dropping to the river. "Oh, my! Look at the time! Looks like we've reached the dock. Fred will want his breakfast and I'd best be getting ready for the tour."

AFTER A QUICK ORIENTATION and a bit more paperwork, their group traveled by tender boat to the pristine dock where a regal-looking man awaited their arrival. Philippe Valmont was perhaps fifty years old. He was impeccably dressed in custom-tailored clothes that bore the Fromagerie Valmont crest in gold embroidery. His salt-and-pepper hair was swept back without a single strand out of place. His mouth was shaped into a rigid smile but the expression seemed forced. It did not quite make it to his eyes. Moreover, there was a look of annoyance and inconvenience in them that suggested he would rather be doing almost anything else besides welcoming them for this tour, on this crisp winter morning. He flipped through the paperwork that Jasper handed him, silently counting the signatures, then the heads in the tender boat.

Only then, when he was satisfied with the numbers, did he step aside so they could all disembark onto his dock.

"Welcome to Fromagerie Valmont," he said once they were all assembled on the dock. His English was perfect but heavily accented. "I am Philippe Valmont, ninth-generation master of the Roquefort tradition. Before we begin, I must reiterate the ground rules and remind you that you have all signed a contract." His gaze swept over them like a general inspecting troops. "No photography. No touching the cheese wheels without permission. No deviation from the tour route. And absolutely no sampling without my explicit approval."

"He's a charmer," Exandra muttered under her breath. The giantess was wearing the same outfit as the day before, minus the beanie. Her hair was blown wild from the wind on the tender boat; tufts of purple and gray stuck out in every direction.

Philippe spun around to face her, and glared up at her with his sharp eyes. "I beg your pardon?"

"I said you're charming," Exandra repeated, louder and more confidently, with an equally forced smile. "We're so lucky to be here today. I'm sure everyone is impressed with your... dedication to tradition."

He regarded her with the kind of look one might give an interesting but ultimately inferior specimen. "Tradition is what separates true craftsmanship from mere production, mademoiselle."

"It's Agent," Exandra corrected. "Agent Exandra Thorne." She held out a hand to shake his, but he ignored it, already continuing on with his presentation.

"Now, if you will follow me." Phillipe Valmont sniffed the air possessively, as if he resented having to share it all with these interlopers.

They entered the fromagerie through a dramatic marble and wrought iron archway carved with the Valmont family crest and descended directly into the caves. Whereas the Swiss fromagerie had been rustic and charming, this place was a temple to controlled perfection. Crystal chandeliers hung from the limestone ceiling, their light reflecting off walls that had been polished smooth and whitewashed. Cheese wheels lined the shelves in absolutely perfect symmetry, each one exactly the same distance from its neighbor.

"It's like a museum," Minerva whispered to Zephyr.

"Or a mausoleum," he whispered back.

Wren's hand strayed to the camera at her hip almost reflexively, drawn by the dramatic lighting. She'd barely touched it when Philippe whirled around.

"Mademoiselle! What did we just say about photography?"

"I'm sorry, I just... It's habit. The lighting in here is extraordinary, and usually for my articles—"

"No. Photographs. No. Exceptions." Each word was bitten off cleanly. "This is your only warning. A second violation and you will be removed from the tour and our lawyers will be in touch."

Wren's jaw tightened, but she tucked the camera away in her bag where she'd be less tempted to touch it. "Understood."

Jasper shot her a sympathetic look. She gave him a tight smile in return.

As they moved deeper into the caves, past chamber after perfectly arranged chamber, Bayard and Exandra drifted toward each other. Minerva watched as they hovered at the edge of the group, whispering like teenagers. When Phillipe stuck his head into a vat of vaguely floral but still powerfully pungent ripening cheese and inhaled deeply, Exandra struggled to suppress a giggle. She buried her head on Bayard's shoulder, shaking with the effort of containing her laughter. Minerva saw tears when Bayard stood on tippy toes to whisper something in Exandra's ear. She could just make out what he said, thanks to her mouse-enhanced hearing.

"Do you think he secretly bathes in the vats when nobody is looking, Exxie?"

"What is so funny?" Phillipe asked.

"Nothing. Nothing at all. I was just helping Agent Thorne with..."

"Something in my eye!" Exandra deadpanned, wiping away a tear.

"Hmph!" Phillippe pinched his lips together tightly and continued on with the tour.

Minerva smiled to herself. Perhaps there was hope for Exandra and Bayard yet.

THE WALKING TOUR concluded in a presentation chamber where a perfect wheel of Roquefort sat displayed on a rotating marble pedestal. It was topped with a tiny jeweled crown that sparkled in the spotlights. As they all took their seats in the gallery, Phillippe launched into a highly technical lecture about *Penicillium roqueforti* cultures, bacterial ratios, and precise humidity requirements. He paused at regular intervals for questions, his tone suggesting that everyone should be taking notes for a final exam. But even Wren had stopped writing things down, both because the subject was so dry and because she feared the legal consequences of paying too close attention as much as she feared getting it wrong.

After ten minutes of Philippe's droning superiority, Bayard gently interjected. "Phillippe? If I may? I thought the group might enjoy the traditional origin story of Roquefort cheese."

Philippe looked momentarily annoyed at the interruption, but waved a hand in permission and stepped aside.

Bayard strode slowly to the podium, already telling the story as he walked. His cane tapped out a lyrical cadence to his tale.

"There's a charming local legend," Bayard began, his voice warm and engaging in contrast to Philippe's lecturing, "about a young shepherd who brought his lunch to work with him. A nice sandwich of bread and fresh cheese. He set it down in one of these caves while he went to tend his flock. But then suddenly he saw a tall, athletic, beautiful woman walking in the fields below."

Bayard paused here and cast a long look at Exandra. Long enough that the agent blushed.

"Naturally, the young shepherd couldn't resist her. So he dropped his crook..." Bayard made a show of dropping his cane to the ground, causing at least a couple of the guests to startle. Phillippe frowned. Bayard waved his hands animatedly and imitated running. "And he ran down the hillside to chase after her."

Beside her, Zephyr nudged Minerva as if to say "Are you catching this?" Minerva smiled and slid her tiny hand into Zephyr's much larger one as Bayard continued the tale.

"When the shepherd returned to the cave weeks later, having forgotten all about his lunch, he found the sandwich was still there, but the cheese had transformed. Blue veins ran through it now, and the taste was unlike anything he'd ever experienced."

"The mold spores were already in the cave," Jasper said, clearly fascinated. "They just needed the right conditions to bloom."

"Exactly." Bayard smiled at him. "The same *Penicillium roqueforti* that grows here naturally, that's been cultivated and maintained for centuries. But I like to think that part of the magic is in the story itself—the accident, the patience, the discovery that sometimes the best things come from letting nature take its course."

His eyes found Exandra's again as he said this last part. She was looking at him, too, and for a moment something passed between them. Recognition, longing, and perhaps the acknowledgement of their own long patience.

"I have a question." Wren raised her hand. "What happened to the girl?"

"Well…" Bayard hemmed as he considered his response. "The story doesn't relate, but I like to think…"

Philippe cleared his throat loudly, interrupting. "Yes, well, although the romantic folklore is charming, it's just a silly story. We should move on now. Let me show you the actual process."

THE (CHEESE) WHEEL OF FORTUNE

*P*hillippe had them all don white lab coats, shoe covers, and hair nets before leading them into the production area where workers were piercing finished wheels with long golden needles, creating channels for air to reach the interior of the cheese.

"These holes allow oxygen to penetrate," Philippe explained. "The *Penicillium roqueforti* is aerobic—it needs air to grow. Without the piercing, you simply have a mild white cheese. With it, you have *Roquefort*." He spoke the name of his beloved cheese with passion and reverence.

They all watched as the workers moved with practiced precision, each wheel receiving exactly forty-two pierces—no more, no less.

"That's so cool," one of the passengers commented. "I've always loved blue cheese. Have you ever tried a bacon gorgonzola burger?"

Phillipe froze, a look of sheer horror on his face. He spun on his heel, turning to face the passenger.

"What was that you just said?" he hissed. The passenger cowered, unsure whether or not to repeat himself. But before he even had a chance to respond, Phillipe went on. "Gorgonzola. You dare to mention this cow filth in my caves? This paste that is so awful they name it after monsters? You know what? I think it is parfait you should combine it with something as terrible as a 'burger,' which is quite possibly the least refined sandwich, from the least refined continent!" He was indignant and only just getting started, Minerva feared. "How dare you even say the name of this inferior cheese here in my temple!"

"I, uh... I'm sorry?" the passenger stammered.

"I think," Bayard intervened, attempting to deescalate the situation, "what my tour group member was trying to say was that your blue cheese is so superior to anything else he's ever tried." He shot a quick look at the passenger, who nodded vigorously, taking the ball and running with it.

"Right, that's exactly what I meant. Gorgonzola... Feh! I would never touch the stuff. I can't believe it's legal to even sell it." He breathed heavily as Phillippe stared at him.

Phillipe flicked a speck of imaginary dust off his jacket. "Yes, well, we all know that the American Ordinaries will eat anything. I cannot say I am the least bit surprised. Rest assured we will not be serving up any monstrous cow products here. Here we have only two types of genuine Roquefort. The regular, and the Yule Cru.

"Would you tell us more about your Yule cheese?" Wren asked, her notebook out again. "What makes that one so special?"

Philippe's entire bearing shifted, becoming even more pompous if that were possible. "Ah. The Yule Roquefort is produced exclusively from the milk of our *magical* sheep. They are the ones you may have seen on the hillside on your way in. These creatures graze exclusively on wildflowers pollinated by magical bees. The result is a cheese with subtle honey notes that perfectly complement the bold blue veins. The flavor infuses the coming year with both a sweetness and a depth that is intoxicating."

"Will we have a chance to taste it?" Wren asked hopefully.

Philippe looked at her as if she'd asked to borrow his crown. "Heavens, no! Absolutely not! The Yule cheese is reserved for magical royalty and certain distinguished families on our worthiness list. It is far too rare and precious for casual sampling by *tourists*." Phillippe looked around the room, eyes lingering a bit too long on Exandra who was openly glaring at him now.

"Worthiness list?" Minerva asked, her tone carefully neutral.

"Families of particular magical distinction, impeccable lineage, significant contributions to our community." Philippe waved his hand dismissively. "We produce only twenty wheels each season. They are all already spoken for."

Exandra rolled her eyes so hard Minerva was surprised they didn't audibly click. She saw the agent catch Bayard's eye behind Phillippe's back. Bayard made a face back at her that indicated they were both on the same page. It was a look that said, "Can you believe this pompous idiot?"

This interaction was so natural, so much like old partners sharing a silent joke. Minerva's heart skipped a beat. Whatever had gone wrong between them, whatever prevented them from speaking their truth, she was certain that underneath it all, they still understood each other perfectly.

"Come," Philippe said. "I will now show you the Yule cheese ripening chamber. You may look, but I cannot stress this enough: Do not touch anything!"

"Are we permitted to breathe?" Exandra mumbled under her breath.

THE YULE CHAMBER was much smaller, more intimate than the main caves. Inside, twenty wheels of cheese rested on special shelves, each one marked with an embossed golden seal pressed into the wax, and a tiny jeweled crown affixed to the seal. Even through the protective wax coating, Minerva could sense something different about these cheeses. There was a glimmer of magic, a radiant warmth that had nothing to do with temperature.

Jasper leaned close, his voice earnest. "Mr. Valmont, what happens to the cheese if one of the families on the list... doesn't want their cheese? Or can't accept it?"

"Impossible," Philippe said flatly. "No one refuses Valmont Yule Roquefort."

"But theoretically—"

"It has never happened. It will never happen." Philippe was already moving away. "Now, let us proceed to the tasting room where you may sample our standard Roquefort. This way."

The group began to follow, but Bayard lingered behind, his bright eyes on those golden-sealed wheels. Something in his expression made Minerva pause, too.

But then Zephyr took her hand, pulling her away. "Coming along, my dear?"

"Yes," she said, but she glanced back over her shoulder once more as she walked through the door.

Bayard had removed his backpack carrier, and was pausing to look inside.

"Just checking on Fred," Bayard said. "He's been napping for the entire tour. I should probably find him some water."

Minerva's stomach growled. She was getting peckish.

BAYARD SLIPPED into the small anteroom off the main tasting room. The space served as a butler's pantry. Bayard had noticed some workers getting their sample platters ready in here earlier. The others were all in the tasting room. Valmont was still talking to the group. He didn't have a lot of time. Bayard carefully lowered Fred's backpack carrier onto the counter. His hands shook as he unzipped it. Fred lay curled in his usual spot, oblivious to the value of the golden-sealed wheel nestled in the compartment below him.

"Sorry, old friend," Bayard whispered. "This will just take a moment."

He looked at the platter of regular cheese waiting to be brought out for the tour group to taste. It held a standard wheel of Valmont Roquefort, perfectly presentable but nowhere near as precious as the Yule cheese. With quick, efficient movements, Bayard removed the standard wheel. He then unwrapped the Yule wheel, and placed it onto the tasting platter, carefully arranging it to look like it had always been there. He then shoved both wrappers and the standard wheel back into the bottom compartment of his backpack.

Fred's eyes opened wide and he stared accusatorily at Bayard.

"Shh," Bayard pleaded. "I know. It stinks. But please, Fred, just—"

"*QUACK!*"

The sound echoed in the small space like a gunshot. Bayard froze, his heart in his throat, waiting for footsteps, for Philippe's outraged voice, for discovery.

But Philippe was still lecturing in the other room, his nasal voice carrying through: "—and the crystallization of the tyrosine amino acids creates that pleasant granular texture, which the uneducated palate often mistakes for—"

No one was coming.

Fred looked up at Bayard with his beady eyes, and if a duck could be said to have expressions, the duck's expression seemed almost knowing. Almost approving of his mischief.

"You understand, don't you?" Bayard whispered, closing the backpack. "Some rules deserve to be broken."

Fred quacked once more, softly this time, and tucked his head back under his wing.

Bayard slipped into the back of the tasting room, hoping that nobody had noticed those few extra moments he'd been gone. Fred's carrier pack was extra heavy against his shoulders. The duck was asleep again, his soft snores barely audible, unconcerned that he'd just been an accessory to a cheese heist.

Bayard's heart hammered at the thought of what he had just done. What on earth had he been thinking? This was an actual theft, not a mere prank. But he regretted nothing. The thought of Philippe's dismissive tone, his snooty "worthiness list," and the way the cheesemaker had looked at Exandra like she didn't have any right to be there...

It had ignited something in Bayard. Quite possibly that same fierce thirst for social justice that had led him to join the Society for the Protection of Natural Magic to begin with.

He was nervous. But he also felt so alive. More alive than he'd felt for years. And what was the worst thing that would happen if he got caught? It was just one wheel of cheese. And he hadn't taken it for himself. He could always play the befuddled old professor card if caught. What would Valmont do? Kick him out and ban him from ever coming back again?

Worth it.

The tasting room, he now saw, was another exercise in controlled perfection. There were about a dozen marble bistro tables, crystal glasses for wine pairings, and carefully placed bowls of palate-friendly accompaniments waiting for Philippe's grand presentation of the Valmont treasure. Bayard spotted some sliced figs, pears, and apples cut into matchsticks, an assortment of nuts, and a chunky compote that looked like quince jam. All that was missing was the actual cheese.

Bayard's mouth watered, remembering the smell as he'd hastily swapped the cheeses in the anteroom. He wiped his hands on his pants one more time, just in case any incriminating crumbles lingered.

The group was still gathered near the countertop while their unctuous host went on about the proper tasting technique.

"Cheese is not simply something to be tasted with your mouth. You must savor it with all six of your senses. Look at it first." Phillipe pantomimed staring lovingly at an invisible wedge of cheese. "Next you must touch it. Gently at first, like a shy lover." He petted his pretend cheese. "And then with passion!" Phillipe clenched two fingers emphatically around the imaginary hunk. "Does she make a sound? Can you hear her squeak? Do not be afraid to press your fingers into her flesh. She will not bite you! Feel how she yields, melting at your touch?"

From the other side of the chamber, Bayard heard a loud snort that he was certain came from Exandra but he dared not look in that direction, lest he succumb to a fit of nervous laughter.

"Next we smell..." Phillipe inhaled long and loud, holding the pretend cheese aloft at arm's length. "And now it is time to put it in your mouth..." Phillippe puckered up like he was about to smooch the cheese.

Touring this facility was such an elite privilege, but Phillipe was so over the top that Bayard was already second guessing his decision to bring the group here. Most of all, he hated the way the wizard cheesemaker looked down his nose at Exandra, like he resented a giantess gaining access to his inner sanctum. As prestigious and exclusive as the place was, Bayard didn't think he'd want to bring another group back.

Jasper caught his eye now and mouthed a question. "*Where did you go?*"

He mouthed "*Water*" and gestured to Fred's backpack.

Jasper nodded, satisfied, and turned his attention back to Wren, who was paying rapt attention.

At long last, Philippe finally, *finally*, went to fetch the cheese from the anteroom. He presented the platter with a flourish, completely unaware he was about to serve contraband Yule cheese to common tourists.

"This is a standard Valmont Roquefort," he announced as he sliced into it and passed the wedges around. "Eight months old, the minimum acceptable age for proper flavor development. Note the even distribution of blue veining, the creamy ivory paste, the—"

But no one was listening anymore because the moment the first person took a bite, everything changed.

"Oh," Wren breathed, her eyes going wide. "Oh, my."

"This is…" Jasper trailed off, staring at the cheese in his hand like it was sentient and might answer back.

Minerva took a small piece, and the moment it touched her tongue, warmth bloomed through her chest. Honey. Wildflowers. Summer days that lasted forever. Every happy memory she'd ever had seemed to surface at once, golden and perfect. She knew this taste. There was something familiar about it. It was right on the tip of her tongue…

"Zippy," she said, turning to her husband with sudden urgent affection. "Have I told you today how much I love you?"

"Only seventeen times," he said, grinning at her with the same dopey expression she wore. "But I'll never tire of hearing it."

Around the table, the effects rippled outward. Someone started giggling. Someone else began philosophizing about the nature of perfection. The air filled with a gentle, dreamy haze.

Wren turned to Jasper, her professional reserve completely dissolved. "I can't believe I've only just noticed your eyes," she said wonderingly. "They're like… like warm amber in sunlight. Have they always been that beautiful?"

Jasper, his face flushed, took her hand. "Your hair is so perfectly braided. And the way you frame your photographs, capturing people in moments of joy... The way you see the world! It's the most beautiful thing I've ever seen. *You're* the most beautiful thing I've ever seen."

"You're so earnest," she said, squeezing his fingers. "So genuinely kind. How did I not fully appreciate this from the moment we met?"

Across the room, Bayard and Exandra had gravitated toward each other like magnets. They grew closer and closer until their hands somehow found and entwined with each other's. Then their eyes locked.

"I'm so happy," Bayard said softly, "that the old gang is back together."

But he wasn't looking at anyone else in the room. He was looking only at her.

"Yes," Exandra breathed, her usual sharp edges completely softened. "Together again."

She lifted their joined hands and pressed them against her chest, over her heart. "I've missed checking in with you. Knowing you'd be there when I called with a question or a request for support."

"I'll always be there. I've never stopped—" Bayard started, but then Philippe's voice shattered the moment.

"*Mon Dieu!*" The fromagier had taken a piece himself, and his face had gone from pleased to confused to absolutely horrified in the space of seconds. "This is... this is the Yule cheese! How did—?"

He rushed from the room, his footsteps echoing in the caves. The group remained in their dreamy haze, still holding hands and staring at each other with new eyes, the dizzying effects of the magical cheese still swirling through their systems.

Philippe returned moments later, pale as milk. "A wheel is missing! Someone has stolen a Yule wheel! This is—" He looked at the platter where they'd all been happily eating. "You've consumed royal cheese! This is a disaster!"

"But it's the most delicious thing I've ever tasted," someone said, still giggly.

"It is so much better than gorgonzola cheese," said another passenger.

"What? Of course it is!" Philippe wrung his hands. "It's made for kings! And now—one of the families on our worthiness list will have to be denied. They've already been expecting it. And this entire wheel is wasted, contaminated by common consumers!"

Wren, still holding Jasper's hand but regaining some of her journalistic clarity, asked, "What are the implications? Who loses their cheese?"

"The Beaumonts of Marseille," Philippe said miserably. "They're always the last family added to the list each year. They'll just have to be removed."

"That seems harsh," Jasper said, his earnestness returning as the cheese effects began to fade. "And you're not really going to throw the rest of this wheel away, are you? Why not share what's left of this wheel with the local villagers? It shouldn't go to waste."

Philippe looked like Jasper had suggested setting fire to the caves. "Share Yule Roquefort with the *village*?"

"Why not?" Jasper's voice was stronger now. "Aren't they the ones who maintain the roads to your fromagerie? Who buy your standard cheese? Who support your business all year long?"

Philippe opened his mouth to object, then closed it. Then opened it again. "I... suppose... that is technically..."

"It seems the kind thing to do," Zephyr added. "And the right thing."

"Very well," Philippe said through gritted teeth. "The remainder of this wheel shall be distributed to the village. But the Beaumonts will still—"

"Actually," Minerva spoke up, her voice clear and calm, "I believe *my* family is on your worthiness list. We enjoy a wheel of your fine cheese every Yule. I used to look forward to it. The Lathrops of Boston?"

The effect was immediate and dramatic. Philippe's entire demeanor shifted like someone had flipped a switch.

"L-l-l-lathrop?" he stuttered, staring at her. "As in descended from the great Flora Lathrop?"

"My great-great-grandmother, yes."

Philippe actually *bowed*. "Madame Lathrop, I had no idea! Your family's contributions to French magical culture are impressive. Why, the preservation spells for the Loire Valley vineyards alone, not to mention the development of—"

"Yes, yes, yes..." Minerva said, a bit impatiently. "I'd like to donate my family's wheel. That way no one else needs to be removed from your list. Just make sure that the rest of this wheel gets shared with the townsfolk."

Philippe stammered, clearly torn between horror at the suggestion and the desire to please someone of Minerva's lineage. "That is... most generous, Madame. I will make sure your wishes are honored."

"Thank you." Minerva turned back to the group, where Zephyr was beaming at her with obvious pride.

Exandra stood apart from the rest of the group, her arms crossed, watching the entire exchange with a tight jaw and narrow eyes. Minerva glanced her way, hoping for perhaps a moment of warmth and connection, but when their eyes met, Exandra's expression was cold as ice.

THE TRIP back to the ship was quiet, everyone still processing the lingering effects of the magical cheese. Jasper and Wren sat close together, not quite holding hands but with their shoulders touching. Minerva and Zephyr walked arm in arm, content. The other passengers murmured softly about the extraordinary experience.

Bayard limped along with Fred's backpack, noticeably lighter now that he'd managed to sneak off and ditch the wheel of regular Roquefort in the melee that followed the initial discovery of the switch. Hopefully someone would notice it in the refrigerator in the butler's pantry before it went bad.

He might burst from the tangle of emotions in his chest. Guilt, satisfaction, fear, defiance, and underneath it all, a fierce joy at having pulled off the switch. He'd acted on impulse, and he'd do it again if he had the opportunity. .

Exandra caught up with him as they boarded the ship.

"That was certainly strange," she said without preamble.

"What was?" Bayard's voice came out higher than intended.

"The switched wheels. It doesn't match the Culture Vulture's pattern at all." She was studying him with those sharp eyes, the ones that had seen through so many lies while evaluating rival operatives in the field. "The other incidents were more destructive. Designed to ruin production. But this? This just felt like... mischief."

"Maybe the Culture Vulture isn't all bad," Bayard said, trying to sound confident. "Perhaps they're just trying to make a point."

Exandra shook her head slowly. "I don't think so. This incident was different. It was almost like..."

She trailed off, her gaze moving past him to where Minerva was coming up the gangplank, and her expression darkened.

"Never mind," she said abruptly. "I'll figure it out. That's what I do."

She walked away before Bayard could respond, leaving him standing there with his backpack reeking of evidence and his heart in his throat. Fred quacked softly and bumped his head against Bayard's hand.

"I know," Bayard whispered. "I'm in way over my head, aren't I?"

Fred just stared at him with those knowing eyes.

IN HER CABIN later that evening, Exandra paced, her mind churning. There were two actual incidents now, counting today's switch and the incident upstream that she knew Bayard had reported to the Society. She'd done her best to make the meltdown at the Swiss Fromagerie look like a real sabotage, something professional and dangerous. Though of course she'd had a plan to save the day before any cheese was harmed. If only Minerva hadn't gotten there first. She still couldn't believe she'd been foiled by a mouse shifter.

But today's incident was different. Mostly because it was *so good*. She wished she'd thought of it first. It was almost playful. Suddenly she found herself rooting for the Culture Vulture, and wishing the villain whose name she'd invented was real.

She thought of Bayard's expression when Philippe had been pontificating about worthiness. The way his jaw had tightened. The way he'd disappeared for those few minutes.

It couldn't have been him, could it?

No. She dismissed the possibility. It was impossible. Bayard wasn't a saboteur. He was careful, methodical, thoughtful, and above all a rule follower. He would never...

CHEDDAR DAYS AHEAD

The moment *The Celestine Queen* crossed into the Cornish airspace above Blythe Meadowsweet's farm, they all felt the change. The sharp December chill that had accompanied them through Switzerland and France simply... evaporated. Warm sunlight flooded the deck, and when Minerva looked down at the countryside below, everything blazed in the glorious technicolor hues of summer.

"We're in the bubble," Bayard explained to the assembled passengers. "Blythe maintains a permanent summer enchantment over her farm. She maintains that happy cows need sunshine year-round, and happy cows make better cheese."

"Sounds a little kooky," someone murmured.

"Perhaps, but at the moment, I'd say delightfully so," Bayard said. He turned his face toward the sun and took a moment to bask in the glorious warming rays.

Several passengers crowded up onto the deck to watch as the ship slowly lowered itself into an oversized pond at the edge of the unusual, sprawling farm. The air temperature was a balmy 72 degrees Fahrenheit, with a light breeze and neither too much nor too little humidity in the air. It was enough to make the group heave a collective sigh of relief. Not that any of them complained about the winter chill in their other tour locations. It was just something that they'd all been braced for. And now there was no longer a reason to brace. On the contrary, Minerva had the sudden and uncharacteristic desire to find herself a hammock to nap in.

The creamery itself looked like it had been plucked from a pastoral painting and given a psychedelic makeover. The main barn was painted in swirling rainbow patterns. Dreamcatchers hung from every available tree branch, and wind chimes fashioned from cow bells created a constant musical backdrop. The cows themselves were bell-less. They wandered freely over the property, sashaying across the patios and through the gardens, tails swishing, haunches swaying. They were completely unconcerned with fences or boundaries.

Barefoot on the muddy banks of the pond, waiting to greet them, stood Blythe Meadowsweet herself. She jumped up and down with childish enthusiasm, waving excitedly as the gangplank was lowered.

"Wow!" Wren exclaimed. Even the normally erudite blogger was at a loss for words.

Blythe was magnificent, one of the most beautiful earth witches that Minerva had ever seen. Her long silver hair flowed loose to her waist, woven through with fresh wild-flowers—daisies, cornflowers, and ethereal sprigs of baby's breath. Her dress was an elaborate patchwork creation in every color imaginable, layered with scarves and shawls that billowed around her like wings. She also wore rings on her fingers and all her toes, multiple beaded and belled necklaces, and a solar bright smile that could have powered a small village.

Blythe never seemed to stop moving. Her natural ebullience kept her spinning, dancing, and flinging her whole self into gratuitous hugs.

"Welcome, welcome, my loves!" she called out, her voice rich and warm. "Come ashore! Don't be shy, pets. The cows won't bite—well, Buttercup might nibble your sleeve, but if she does, rest assured she means it affectionately."

As if on cue, a golden-brown cow ambled over and nuzzled Jasper, who went pale and froze in place.

"That's my girl," Blythe cooed, scratching the cow behind her ears. "Showing our guests proper Cornish hospitality, aren't you, darlin'?"

Bayard approached with Fred's carrier, and Blythe's face lit up like she'd just discovered a hoard of buried treasure.

"You must be Bayard Fontaine!" She practically floated toward him, her scarves trailing. "Oh, but the photographs don't do you justice, do they? Such distinguished features. And these eyebrows!" She reached up—actually reached up with both hands—and touched his face, turning it side to side. "Like little expressive clouds of wisdom, they are. Your aura is divine, too. The soul of a poet and the mind of a scientist. Quite a rare combination." Blythe licked her lips like she meant to devour him.

Bayard blinked, clearly caught off guard. "I, uh, thank you? This is a beautiful operation you've—"

"And this hair!" Blythe's curious fingers moved on to Bayard's head, combing through his crazy white fluff of a mane. " I love how unabashed it is! Wild, yet distinguished. And so soft. Like spun moonlight, dear heart. You must tell me your secrets. Do you use jojoba oil?"

"Just an Ordinary shampoo..." Bayard laughed nervously, attempting to edge away.

Behind them, Exandra stripped off her parka and balled her hands into fists. She made a sound that might charitably have been described as a cough. But it actually sounded much more like a possessive growl to Minerva.

"Blythe, this is Agent Exandra Thorne," Bayard said, trying once more to step back politely, but Blythe stepped along with him. Her hands were still tangled in his hair and she wound herself against him like a vine. "She's investigating—"

"Oh, aren't you tall!" Blythe commented, barely glancing up at Exandra. "Quite striking. I hope you can sew. Must be tough to find clothes. Now, Bay... May I call you that? I can't wait to show you around the Creamery. I have a feeling you'll really *get* the artistry and love that's gone into this place. You must sit right beside me for the workshop."

"Well, I, uh... I mean... that is... we...." Bayard struggled to find the words to explain that his first duty was toward the group. He wasn't accustomed to being fawned over and he wasn't sure he liked it.

"Get. Off. Him." Exandra poked Blythe in the shoulder. "Can't you see you're making him uncomfortable? Give the poor guy a little space."

"Oops. My bad. I'm just a hands-on kind of witch." Blythe shrugged. "I can't help myself."

Bayard stumbled a bit, catching himself with his cane as Blythe reluctantly released him.

"No, that's okay, I just needed a moment to get my bearings." Bayard tried to smooth over the situation. They were scheduled to be here for another two and a half hours. He didn't want things to get awkward.

A moment later, she was linking her arm back through Bayard's.

"Why didn't you say you needed help getting your bearings, silly? Let me give you a quick tour. You'll get those bearings back in a jiffy. Hurry, now! We're running late and we have to get all the Yule cheese wrapped before nightfall."

Exandra moved to follow them, but no matter where she positioned herself, Blythe somehow outmaneuvered her, standing between Bayard and the agent, creating a barrier.

"Everyone is welcome to join us, of course," Blythe called over her shoulder. "So long as you limit your energy to good vibes only. Here at Meadowsweet Creamery, we have zero tolerance for bad vibes. Don't make me perform a chakra alignment on you!"

With this statement, she shook a warning finger at Exandra.

Exandra's jaw clenched so hard, Minerva worried she might crack a tooth.

"Shall we follow them?" Zephyr offered his arm to Minerva with an amused smile.

"I do think we'd better," Minerva answered. "I'm a little worried about Exandra."

THE INTERIOR of the main creamery was chaotic, yet organized at the same time.

Traditional copper vats sat alongside the modern equipment, all of it decorated with painted flowers, suns, moons, and peace signs. A cadre of small, stocky men with elaborately braided beards moved efficiently through the space, ushering the production along.

Dwarves, Minerva recognized. They all wore tie-dyed work clothing, clog-like sandals, and matching scowls.

"Those are my special helpers," Blythe explained, still clinging to Bayard's arm. "They've been with me for forty years! They understand cheese the way I understand sunshine—it's in their bones."

One of the dwarves, a grizzled fellow with a bright orange beard, stared ominously at Bayard as they passed. So much for good vibes only. Bayard shuddered.

"Now, then," Bayard said, gently extracting himself from Blythe's creeping grasp under the pretense of addressing the group. "Who wants to learn a little more about cheese production?"

Jasper's hand was the first one that shot up.

"Thank you, Jasper," Bayard smiled wryly, before continuing with the lesson. "Traditional cheddar-making involves a process called cheddaring. It involves stacking and turning the curds repeatedly to achieve the proper texture and acidity. But what makes Meadowsweet Creamery's cheddar so special is the cloth-binding process. I'm sure the group would love to hear more of the details directly from *you*, Ms. Meadowsweet."

"Oh, but you explain it so well, Bay-Bay..." Blythe sighed, booping his nose. She moved to stand close beside him again, but before she could get there, Exandra positioned herself between them. Undeterred, Blythe stepped directly in front of the giant agent and placed her hand possessively on Bayard's shoulder, forcing Exandra to choose between stepping awkwardly to the side or colliding with her.

Minerva caught Zephyr's eye and had to suppress a laugh. This was getting ridiculous.

"The, ummmm... cloth-binding...," Bayard continued. He stepped back a pace and used his cane to create a pocket of air between himself and their clingy hostess. "The cloth allows the cheese to breathe during aging, creating a more complex flavor profile than wax or plastic wrapping."

"But it's not just any cloth," Blythe interjected in a singsong voice, finally focused on something other than Bayard. "Come, my pets, let me show all you the wonders of the wrapping room. This is where the real magic happens. Magic that I'm counting on all of you to be a part of!"

She led them to the vast barn that had been converted into a makeshift workshop. Long tables covered in brown paper stretched the length of the space, and hanging from clotheslines crisscrossing the ceiling were yards and yards of muslin cloth, dyed in every color of the rainbow.

"We dye all the muslin ourselves," Blythe explained, "using natural vegetable pigments. Beetroot for the reds, turmeric for the golds, indigo for the blues. Each batch is unique, and each carries a special blessing for the cheese it will eventually swaddle."

The cloth swayed gently in the warm breeze from the barn's open windows, creating a mesmerizing display of color and light.

"We made these rainbow patterns specifically for the Yule cheeses," Blythe continued, moving to one of the tables. "The different colors bring different blessings—warmth, harmony, abundance, and joy. When our cheese is served on a Yule ploughman's platter, those blessings infuse the whole meal."

On the table lay the wrapping materials that their group would be using in the workshop. Smaller squares of precut tie-dyed muslin, bundles of cinnamon sticks, sprigs of olive wood, containers of edible glitter for sprinkling, and spools of string to bind it all together.

"The final touch," Blythe said, "is a triple-blessed silk ribbon, also naturally dyed. There's a batch curing in the sunlight right now." She gestured toward the windows where a clothesline was visible outside, flowing ribbons dancing in the breeze. "Tonight you will all help us wrap the Yule order—our most important delivery of the season."

"It's so beautiful," Wren said, her camera out. "May I photograph it?"

"Oh, no, doll," Blythe said apologetically. "The magic in the dyes is very temperamental. Camera flashes can disrupt the blessings. I'm afraid you'll have to rely on your words for this one."

Wren looked disappointed but nodded.

Bayard was still trying to regain his professional equilibrium. "The rainbow cheddar itself is aged for exactly nine months in Blythe's caves, where it develops a range of flavors that represent the full spectrum of cheddar possibilities. You get sharp and mellow notes as well as earthy and bright ones, all coexisting beautifully."

"Just like you, dear heart," Blythe said, stroking his cheek. "Such a beautiful balance of qualities you have."

This time, Exandra's attempt to move between them resulted in her hip checking the table, sending several cinnamon sticks rolling across the floor.

"Oops, pardon me," Exandra muttered, dropping to retrieve them, her face flushed with frustration.

"Let me help you, Exandra." Minerva bent down to assist her, their eyes meeting briefly. Understanding passed between them and Exandra's expression flickered with something like gratitude before the defensive walls slid back into place.

"Shall we all proceed to the tasting?" Blythe suggested. "I've prepared a proper ploughman's lunch for you all to enjoy out in the orchard. There's cheddar with crusty bread, my own pickles, a bit of ham, and some lovely apples from my trees."

As the group followed Blythe out toward the sunny orchard, Bayard lingered behind to catch his breath. He sighed a deep sigh of relief. So far, so good. Nothing had gone wrong during their visit to the Meadowsweet Creamery.

But then he froze, a terrible thought occurring to him.

No incident and nothing going wrong meant that Exandra might wrap up her investigation and leave. And he still hadn't summoned the courage to tell her how he felt about her.

The thought made his chest tighten with something like panic.

ACTIONS SPEAK LOUDER THAN CURDS

The picnic was set up outside under a pergola covered in flowering vines that definitely shouldn't have been blooming in December, but they were nevertheless heavy with blossoms. Tables groaned with food. There were thick slices of rainbow cheddar that showed streaks of color through the pale creamy slabs, crusty bread still warm from the oven, gherkins and pepperoncini that sparkled in their jars.

"Now, then, my loves," Blythe announced, "help yourselves to the feast while I pop back to the Creamery to coordinate our schedule with my helpers. The dwarves get a bit testy if I don't give them lots of attention and precise timelines."

She disappeared back toward the workrooms, though not before giving Bayard's shoulder one last squeeze.

Over at the picnic table, Zephyr was explaining the components of a proper ploughman's lunch to an interested group of the passengers. Wren and Jasper stood together near the drinks table, away from the group, and Bayard noticed they were actually having a real conversation, not stilted or nervous, just two people genuinely enjoying each other's company. He was happy for the two of them, and a bit jealous as well. If only things could be that easy with him and Exandra again.

Bayard set Fred's carrier down next to Minerva. "Could you keep an eye on Fred for me? I just need to check something in the barn. The uh... ventilation... looked off earlier."

It was a terrible excuse. Exandra's eyes narrowed with suspicion.

But she was also standing suddenly. "You know what?" she said to Zephyr, "I should do a perimeter check while everyone's distracted. Make sure the premises are secure. I'd hate for there to be another incident."

They moved in opposite directions, neither making eye contact with the other, but both heading toward different sides of the barn.

BAYARD SLIPPED into the barn through a side door, his heart thudding away. The wrapping room was still empty. The colorful muslin swayed gently overhead, casting rainbow shadows across the tables.

He knew what he was about to do was wrong. He knew it was destructive and childish and went against everything he'd spent his career protecting. But the thought of Exandra leaving, of having no reason to stay, of losing this precious opportunity with her, was more than he could bear.

His hands shook as he reached up and grabbed the first piece of muslin.

It came down easily, the fabric soft and ever so slightly damp. He shoved it into a drawer under one of the worktables. Then another. And another. Working quickly now, his heart pounding, he tore down the carefully dyed cloths and stashed them anywhere he could find space. In drawers, in cabinets, behind bales of hay.

I'll put them back later, he told himself. *This isn't permanent. Just enough to cause a delay. Just enough to keep her here.*

At the opposite end of the barn, Exandra snuck inside through the stable.

She'd told herself she was just checking the perimeter. Looking for signs of any potential interlopers, if not for an actual Culture Vulture. She was still doing her job.

But the truth—the truth she could barely admit to herself —was that she was *furious*. Furious and jealous of Blythe Meadowsweet for touching *her* Bayard. Not that she had any right to think of him that way. She was also furious with Bayard for not seeming to mind the fawning attention. He'd seemed perfectly content to let the beautiful witch drool all over him like he was a hunk of her psychedelic cheese. And most of all, Exandra was furious with herself for caring so much when she had no claim on him, no right to be possessive, no reason to feel this burning jealousy except—

Except she *loved* him.

She had always loved him. Would always love him. And would never be able to have him.

The rage that this thought unleashed was sudden and fierce. Her hands found the nearest square of hanging muslin and tore it down. Then another. She stamped them on the dirt floor, grinding the carefully dyed fabric under her boots, selfishly ruining hours of work because she couldn't have what she wanted and it just wasn't *fair*.

BAYARD AND EXANDRA worked their way toward each other through the vast barn, each consumed by their own guilt and desperation and grief, separated only by layers of hanging fabric.

Bayard grabbed another cloth, shoving it behind the rack of brown wrapping paper. Exandra tore down three more squares, crumpling them in her fists.

Bayard pushed past a curtain of orange and gold.

Exandra ducked under swaying squares of blue and green.

The rainbow light filtering through the muslin created an otherworldly atmosphere, turning everything soft and surreal.

They were each clearing a path, getting closer to each other.

Closer.

And closer.

And then, they were standing face to face, both reaching for the same square of purple cloth that cast them both in violet light.

For a long moment, they just stared at each other, frozen.

"What on earth are you doing?" Exandra whispered.

"Maybe you want to tell me what you are doing first?" Bayard shot back.

They looked long and hard at each other, neither brave enough to fully confess their wrongdoing. At last, Exandra broke the silence.

"Oh, gods," Exandra said, her voice breaking. "Bayard, what are we—"

"I was investigating," he said quickly. "I found evidence of tampering. Someone's been in here, and I was trying to—"

"Oh! Me, too," she said, seizing on the excuse. "I found evidence. Of tampering. That's why I was—"

They both knew they were lying. They both knew the other one knew, too.

But admitting the truth meant admitting a great deal more, and neither of them was quite brave enough for that yet.

"We need to fix this," Bayard said softly. "Before anyone sees."

"Yes." Exandra was already moving, gathering and shaking out the clothes she'd trampled. "The dwarves will be back soon."

They worked together in silence at first, rehanging the muslin, smoothing out the wrinkles, retrieving the pieces Bayard had hidden. Their hands brushed occasionally, and each time they did, it generated a small electric shock.

"I've missed this," Bayard admitted. He reached up to clip a yellow square back onto the line. "Working in the field together. Being partners."

Exandra paused, a green cloth in her hands. "Yes. I've missed it, too."

"Exandra, I need to tell you something—"

"No. Bayard, let me go first. There's something I have to—"

"*QUAAAAAACK!*"

The sound was pure panic, coming from outside. Fred's voice, high and distressed, followed by a deeper, more aggressive quacking.

They dropped everything and ran.

CHEDDAR LATE THAN NEVER

The scene outside was chaos.

Fred was running—or rather, waddling—at top speed across the farmyard, his wings flapping frantically. Behind him, moving with surprising agility for her size, was the largest duck Minerva had ever seen. She had to be twice Fred's size, with glossy brown feathers and an expression that could only be described as determined devotion.

"*Quack quack quack!*" Fred was frantic, flying straight for the clothesline where the silk ribbons were hanging to dry.

"Fred, no!" Bayard shouted, but it was too late.

Fred attempted to fly under the low-hanging line, but his anxiety made him clumsy. He crashed directly into one of the flimsy support poles.

The entire clothesline swayed, tilted, and then collapsed.

Dozens of hand-dyed silk ribbons, each one blessed and cured in the magical sunlight, flew into the air. They scattered everywhere like a rainbow explosion. They flew across the yard, into the cow pasture, up into the trees, and wrapped themselves around the dreamcatchers.

"Over here, Fred! I've got you!" Exandra called, holding up his carrier. Fred dove into the proffered backpack, gratefully and speedily taking refuge in the safe space.

The larger duck suddenly stopped her pursuit, looking confused about where her target had gone.

"Oh, no," Blythe breathed, emerging from the Creamery with the dwarves behind her. "Oh, no, no, no. The ribbons! The Yule order!"

Exandra was already moving, holding a ruffled and indignant Fred in her arms. "You need to get your duck under control!" she snapped at Blythe.

"I'm not sure what you mean by that. We don't 'control' anyone or anything here at Meadowsweet Farms," Blythe protested. "Helga's just friendly. She doesn't mean any harm."

"Friendly?" Exandra clutched Fred protectively to her chest. The little duck was shaking in his carrier, and she worried that he'd been traumatized by the incident. "That's harassment. Fred made his lack of interest perfectly clear. Like cheesemaker, like duck," she added angrily under her breath.

The dwarves surveyed the disaster with grim expressions. The grizzled one who'd glared at Bayard earlier stepped forward.

"This is a catastrophe," he said, his deep voice thick with accusation. "Those ribbons took three days to dye and bless. Without them, the Yule cheeses can't be properly wrapped. It's our most important order of the year…"

"I'll help," Bayard volunteered. "We'll all help. We can gather them, surely—"

The dwarf's eyes narrowed. "Convenient that you were just in the wrapping room. Alone."

"I was checking the ventilation," Bayard said, but he could hear how weak it sounded.

"Were you, now?" The dwarf crossed his arms. "And did the ventilation require you to touch our carefully hung muslin?"

Bayard's face went pale.

Exandra stepped forward, still holding Fred. "He was investigating. At my request. There have been incidents at other fromageries—sabotage. We're trying to prevent the same thing from happening here."

"Seems to have happened anyway," another dwarf muttered.

"Enough," Blythe said, though her usual cheerfulness was strained. "We have to stay positive. Arguing won't retrieve the ribbons. We have—" She checked a pocket watch hanging from one of her many necklaces "—eight hours before the final wrapping must be done." She sighed heavily. "I hate to be a downer, but If we don't complete the order by midnight, the blessings might not hold up properly."

"Then we'd better get started," Minerva said, stepping

forward. "All of us. Come along, everyone. We need everyone's help. It's for a sort of scavenger hunt."

THE RIBBONS HAD SCATTERED across the entire farm, caught by the perpetual summer breeze. Some were draped artistically over fence posts. Some were tangled in tree branches. One particularly adventurous purple ribbon had wrapped itself around Buttercup the cow, who hated to part with her new accessory.

The tour group fanned out across the property, calling out whenever they spotted a flash of color. The dwarves got to work cleaning and pressing the recovered ribbons. Blythe even convinced the cows to help, and the animals proved surprisingly effective at nuzzling out the ones that were caught in the tall grass.

Wren climbed a tree to retrieve a stray cluster of green and gold ribbons, laughing as they fanned out behind her in the breeze. From the ground, Jasper watched her, wishing he had a camera. He framed her with his hands and took the picture in his head, determined to capture and remember Wren perched in the branches, her face lit with genuine joy, the endless summer sunshine making everything glow.

She looked down and saw him, and instead of being annoyed or self-conscious, she just smiled wider. "Did you get a good one?"

"Perfect," he said softly.

Back in the picnic area, Minerva and Zephyr took over hosting duties, making sure the guests who weren't looking for the ribbons, or were taking a break from the hunt, were well fed and entertained. They devised a point system, based on the ribbon colors and lengths, and quickly came up with rewards for the passengers who collected the most ribbons. These would have to be distributed back on the ship. The awards included a gift certificate for The Squeaky Wheel, a photography lesson with Wren, a self-defense training session with Exandra, and a cooking class with Jasper.

"You see," Minerva explained, setting out more bread and cheese, "a proper ploughman's platter is about teamwork. The sharp cheddar, the sweet pickles, the crusty bread, the crisp apple. Each element supporting the others. No single flavor overwhelming. Just... harmony."

She glanced toward the farmyard where Bayard was using magic to summon ribbons from high tree branches, while Exandra interrogated the dwarves about any other potential hiding places, and she smiled.

By the time the sun began to lower, they'd recovered nearly all the ribbons. Bayard and several dwarves stood in the center of the farmyard, wands raised, ready to try one last spell of return.

"*Reveni ribbons,*" they chanted together.

The last few ribbons streamed through the air from every direction—red and gold and blue and green and purple and orange. A few of them were tattered but still swimming through the air like painted eels toward the outstretched hands of the waiting dwarves. It was a beautiful, magical, and strange sight to behold.

The grizzled dwarf counted the haul now, his expression slowly softening. "Ninety-seven out of one hundred. We can make it work."

"And Buttercup can keep her bow! Thank you, everyone." Blythe said, addressing the whole group. Her clingy flirtatiousness was subdued at last, replaced with gratitude. "You've saved our Yule order. The families who've been waiting all year—they'll be able to have their blessed cheese after all."

She looked at Bayard, and this time her touch on his arm was brief, respectful. "You're a good man, Bayard Fontaine. Your friend is lucky to have you."

Bayard's throat was tight. "Thank you for your hospitality."

Blythe turned toward Exandra next. The agent still held Fred protectively, the carrier strapped to her chest. She hadn't set him down the entire time they were hunting for the ribbons, not even for an instant.

"I've had a heart-to-heart with Helga," Blythe confided. "And she wants Fred to know she's sorry. She only wanted to play, but she understands now that she needs to be more gentle with newcomers, and ask for their consent before making inappropriate advances. My apologies as well. It's not entirely her fault. She's an odd duck."

Exandra coughed.

"We'll keep a closer eye on her," the grizzled dwarf said to Exandra. But he wasn't looking around for Helga when he said it. He was placing a protective hand on Blythe's hip, and gazing up at her with adoration.

BACK ON BOARD *The Celestine Queen*, Exandra was loath to hand Fred back to Bayard. She stroked his head gently, murmuring to him.

"You're all right now," she whispered. "No more unwanted attention from crazy old mallards."

Bayard was walking beside her.

"Thank you," he said gratefully. "For protecting him. For... everything." For once, when he gently touched her shoulder, she didn't pull away.

"He's a good duck," Exandra said, not quite meeting his eyes. "I just want him to feel safe and happy and like he can be himself. He deserves better."

They both knew she wasn't only talking about Fred.

AS CORNWALL FADED behind them and the eternal summer bubble gave way to a normal winter evening, Minerva and Zephyr headed to the library. He was planning on playing a few rounds of solitaire and she'd collected papers and pens with which to make the gift certificates for the ribbon hunt winners.

Neither of them could resist a bit of gossip about their day.

"Well," she said, "today was certainly educational."

"Indeed. I learned several interesting things today." Taking a brief break from the cards, he counted on his fingers. "One: Our friends are both saboteurs. Two: They're both lousy at it. Three: They're both desperately in love with each other and completely unable to say so. And four: Never underestimate the chaos a lovesick odd duck can cause."

"All accurate observations." Minerva leaned against him. "But the question is whether you think we should do anything about it?"

"Items one through three? I'm not sure yet. Item four?" He smiled. "I think Fred's earned hazard pay. Perhaps an extra serving of frozen peas."

BELOW DECK, Bayard sat in his cabin with Fred nestled beside him, both of them exhausted. The small duck seemed fully recovered from his ordeal, though he kept falling asleep with one eye open.

"I nearly confessed everything today," Bayard whispered to Fred. "Twice. Once in the barn, once after you got attacked. But the moments passed, and I couldn't find the words."

Fred quacked softly, sympathetically.

"I know." Bayard hung his head in shame. "I'm such a coward."

ALL WARM AND MELTY INSIDE

Minerva woke to the sound of wind howling against the portholes and ice crystals forming patterns against the glass. She stretched luxuriously under the thick duvet, warm and content, and reached for Zephyr's hand. He was already awake, propped up against the headboard with his reading glasses perched on his nose, perusing the daily newsletter that was slipped under their door.

"Good morning, my dear," he said, kissing the top of her head. "It seems we're in for a proper winter's day."

"Are we still moving?"

"Indeed. *The Celestine Queen's* stabilization charms are working so perfectly that you'd never know we're currently flying through a snowstorm." He held up the parchment. "According to *The Current*, today is a travel day. No stops, no tours. But we'll be kept busy. The crew has organized a full day of holiday activities aboard the ship."

Minerva sat up, intrigued. "Oh? What sort of activities?"

"Let's see… There's a book exchange in the library, based on the Icelandic 'Jolabokaflod' tradition. That's going on all day. There will be a cookie decorating session in the dining room, a holiday market in the atrium with vendors selling handcrafted goods, and…" He paused to smack his lips. "This sounds lovely. Staff will be passing by with hot glühwein and mulled cider all day."

"That does sound perfect for a snowy day," Minerva said, already imagining curling up in a corner of the library with a new book and a hot drink.

"They're also featuring demonstrations throughout the day. Ornament making, traditional Yule crafts, that sort of thing." Zephyr folded the newsletter and set it aside. "I'm rather looking forward to a leisurely day. No rushing about, no cheese emergencies."

Minerva laughed. "One can hope, but the day is young, dear!"

BY MID-MORNING, the atrium had been transformed into an enchanting winter market. Strings of lights crisscrossed the ceiling, and small wooden booths lined the perimeter, each one draped in evergreen garlands and twinkling with fairy lights. The air smelled of cinnamon, cloves, and pine.

Each booth displayed different traditional handmade wares: carved ornaments, knitted scarves and mittens, beeswax candles, small wooden toys, and lacy paper snowflakes and lanterns. Cruise ship staff circulated with trays full of charming souvenir mugs filled with hot beverages. It was difficult to choose between the glühwein, mulled cider, hot chocolate with peppermint, and spiced tea.

At one end of the atrium, a long table was set up for cookie decorating. Guests were free to choose from the stacks of either plain gingerbread men or round sugar cookies as their canvas.

And then it was time to start embellishing!

Children and adults alike clustered around, wielding icing of every color and sprinkles of many shapes and sizes with varying degrees of skill, enthusiasm, and stickiness tolerance.

On the other end of the atrium, Jasper was browsing at a booth with snow globes for sale, each one more intricate than the last. The artist, an elderly wizard with paint-stained fingers, was explaining the symbolism behind various designs.

"This one," he said, holding up a delicate glass sphere with a tiny jeweled camera surrounded by stars, "represents the act of capturing memories in your mind. The light we save from everyday moments might otherwise fade, were it not for the camera of the imagination."

Jasper stared at it, thinking of Wren framed between the tree branches, ribbons streaming out behind her. That moment he'd captured only in his head.

"It's perfect! I'll take it," he said impulsively.

The vendor wrapped the snow globe carefully in tissue paper and tucked it into a small box. Jasper slipped the box into his jacket pocket, his heart hammering. He wasn't sure when, or even if, he'd have the courage to give it to Wren. But having it at the ready felt important somehow as he crossed back over to the cookie table where she was snapping photos.

"I feel like I've stepped inside a cheesy Yule card," Wren mused when he snuck up beside her. She was enjoying capturing the warm glow of candlelight on so many happy faces. She pretended she hadn't noticed Jasper shopping in the snow globe booth. She didn't want to get her hopes up. But she'd told him that she collected snow globes, and he seemed to have a spring in his step that he definitely hadn't had a few minutes ago. Moreover, he was smiling like he was quite pleased with himself.

"Hey, would you like to decorate a cookie with me?" Jasper asked, then immediately looked embarrassed. "I mean, if that's not too childish. We could just go browse at the market instead, if you prefer. Or—"

"No, no! Are you kidding? I'd *love* to do a cookie with you," Wren said simply. Jasper's face lit up.

"Great! Let me just tell Bayard where I'll be for a bit."

When Jasper returned to the cookie-decorating table, Wren had set their cookie aside. Instead she was helping a small girl who'd gotten frosting all over her hands and was close to tears.

"Here you go, Lisbeth," Wren said gently, handing the child a wet cloth. "No harm done. And look, you can make that squiggle a part of the design. See? Now it totally looks like snow."

The girl's face brightened, and she attacked the cookie with renewed enthusiasm.

Jasper watched Wren, so patient and kind. She made him feel all warm and glowy inside. Part of it was the magical holiday ambiance. But a larger part of it was Wren's natural charm. She grinned at him now. He noticed she had sprinkles stuck to her cheek.

He reached out to brush them off, then tasted one. "Mmmm! Chocolate freckles are the best."

"I have no idea how those got there." Wren giggled. Then she changed the subject. "Have you seen Fred's new sweater?"

"No?" Jasper cocked his head. Come to think of it, he hadn't seen Fred all morning. "Where is the little guy?"

"He's over there, modeling for his supper. Putting on quite the show! Who knew what a ham that little bird was!"

She pointed toward the knitwear booth, where Fred was waddling self-importantly between the displays, modeling his newest wardrobe acquisition: a tiny cream-colored sweater with an embroidered cheese wheel emblazoned across the back. He paused dramatically in front of a group of guests, then pivoted on his webbed foot, waddling back around the tiny booth for a second pass.

"He's absolutely precious," the vendor cooed, straightening Fred's collar. "I couldn't have found a better model for my line. Who could resist such a cute duck in a handknit sweater?"

Fred quacked proudly and continued his circuit of the market, accepting compliments and treats from admirers.

"Just let me know if he gives you any trouble," Wren said. "Bayard asked me to keep an eye on him while he's in a meeting.

"Oh, he's no bother at all," the vendor said. "I should probably be offering him a salary!"

"All right, then!" Wren turned back to Jasper, who was still watching her with that goofy "I-have-a-secret" grin.

"About that cookie..." He held up a tube of frosting and a bowl of rainbow colored sprinkles. "I hope you don't mind getting a little messy!"

"Bring it on!" She smiled.

SLICE OF LIFE

The cold punched like a physical blow when Bayard stepped outside. Wind whipped snow across the deck, and the temperature had to be well below freezing. But Zephyr was already there, leaning against the railing, his face turned up to the storm.

"Bit bracing, being out here in the storm, isn't it?" Zephyr said as Bayard joined him.

"Bracing is one word for it," Bayard agreed, his breath forming clouds. He had to shout to be heard. "Foolhardy might be another."

"Ah, but sometimes you need the cold to think clearly." Zephyr pulled out a silver flask and offered it to Bayard. "Medicinal. Against the chill."

Bayard took a grateful sip of the brandy, smooth and warming. He handed it back, and they stood in companionable silence for a moment, watching the snow swirl around them.

"You wanted to talk," Zephyr said. It wasn't a question.

Bayard sighed, his shoulders sagging. "Was I that obvious?"

"Only to someone who's known you for the better part of a century." Zephyr took another sip from the flask. "I presume this is about Exandra?"

"When isn't it about Exandra?" Bayard's laugh was bitter. "I thought... when you retired, when you found Minerva again and told her how you felt, I thought perhaps I might find that courage, too. That I might tell her..."

"Tell her what?" Zephyr's eyes were a clear, true blue.

He was going to make Bayard say it.

"That I love her. That I've always loved her. That every day without her feels incomplete." The words tumbled out of Bayard, raw and desperate. "But I can't seem to make myself do it, Zeph. Agent Thorne deserves so much better than a broken-down old academic with a limp and a duck."

"Broken-down?" Zephyr's eyebrows rose. "Bay, you're one of the most accomplished people I know. Your work in cultural preservation has saved hundreds of traditions from extinction. You speak six languages fluently, and I'm pretty sure you could outpace me in a footrace. With or without the cane."

"But she doesn't want that version of me," Bayard interrupted. "She wants the man I was supposed to be. The young, promising, agile field agent. The partner who could keep up with her. The wizard who wasn't... damaged."

Zephyr was quiet for a long moment. When he did speak, his voice took on a gentler tone.

"You know," he said, "you've never told me exactly what happened that day. All I know is that one moment we were the three musketeers tearing up the field together, and the next you were manning a desk in the home office."

"I messed everything up." Bayard's hands tightened on his cane.

"You had an accident. We were still a team. Just a different kind of team. And I'd really love to hear the real story of what happened in the gorge that night." Zephyr put a hand on Bayard's shoulder. "If you want to tell it to me, that is."

Bayard sighed. It was so long ago. Nobody who might have cared was even around anymore. What did he have to lose? He gripped the railing tight with both hands. The air was metallic in his nostrils, and he didn't want to drag it out. So he launched right into it.

"We were so young. So stupid, Agent Thorne and I. We snuck off together—we weren't supposed to, of course, but Exandra wanted to practice boulder rolling in the river, and I relished any chance to impress her with my water wielding skills." He laughed humorlessly. "Neither of us anticipated the landslide."

"Wait... Agent Thorne was there with you that day?" Zephyr's eyes grew wide. "I thought you'd gone AWOL alone."

"That was the story we settled on, Exandra and I. There was no point in both of us getting kicked out of the program." Bayard shook his head sadly. "But the truth is that we went down to the gorge together. Even though we'd been explicitly told to avoid it." Bayard rubbed his hands together and Zephyr held out the flask for his old friend to take another swig. Bayard took it and resumed the story a moment later.

"She was rolling boulders and I was dodging them, showing off, manipulating the water to carry me up and over the stones. I made it freeze into ridiculous shapes, lifting me up and out of the way—a chariot, a rocket, an ice dragon—anything to make her laugh. I was so distracted by her laughter, I didn't notice the current shifting as the river rose. I didn't even sense the danger until it was too late." His voice dropped. "It all happened so fast. The shockwave, and the hillside crumbling. I slipped and fell at the worst moment. Exandra's boulder took me down like a bowling pin and then the river of mud came rushing through. It pulled me deep under the rushing river and smashed me against the rocks. Thankfully, I was unconscious by then. I don't remember it. But I know I would have drowned if Exandra hadn't dove in after me. She saved my life, Zeph. "

"My gods!" Zephyr held a hand to his cheek, eyes wide with disbelief. "What were the two of you thinking?"

"We thought we were invincible." Bayard shrugged. "Like I said, young and stupid. I knew as soon as I came to that something was seriously wrong with my leg. I didn't want Exxie getting in trouble. I made her swear not to tell them the truth about where we'd been, that we'd both snuck off together. We concocted a whole story. She told them she'd been out for a run and found me on the riverbank. She actually won a service award for carrying me to the infirmary so promptly. You know the rest. The Society promoted the two of you to field work shortly after that. Rightly so. You were both brilliant, brave, exactly what they needed. And I…" He gestured to his cane. "Even after months of healing, physical therapy, and learning to walk again, I was deemed unfit for field duty. Fortunately, they offered me a supporting role, doing research and running scenarios from the home office instead."

"Which you excelled at." Zephyr's voice was gruff. "You always said you didn't mind."

"I didn't mind it, actually." Bayard took another sip from the offered flask. "That's the irony. I've always been a bit of a bookworm at heart. Doing research and solving puzzles was always my favorite part of our training. But do you know what Exandra said to me, the day they told us? She said, 'I'm so sorry. This is all my fault. You must want to *die*.' And that she wouldn't blame me for hating her."

"It wasn't her fault," Zephyr said firmly.

"Not at all. I didn't hate her. And I certainly didn't want to die," Bayard said. "I was actually pretty glad to still be of service. I fancied myself the brains of the operation. There to watch over and keep the two of you safe. But that's not how Exxie saw it. She could barely look at me and when she did, all she saw was a failure. A failure of a broken man that was all her fault. She still sees me that way."

The wind howled around them, snow stinging their faces. Neither man moved.

"Come on, Bay, you don't actually think that's how she sees you?" Zephyr asked.

"Don't you?"

"We couldn't have done half of what we did in the field without you being back in the home office to support us," Zephyr said slowly. "I've never thought less of you because of that cane and I don't think for one minute that Exandra sees you as damaged goods, either."

"What makes you say that?" Bayard leaned against the rail and rested his head in his hands.

"Well, for starters, she's *here*. Right now. On this cruise. Investigating a case that, if we're being honest, seems like an oddly timed excuse to keep her near you."

"She came because she has some misguided notion that she's got to protect me."

"Or..." Zephyr was beginning to get exasperated with his friend. "Hear me out. Maybe she's here because she still wants to be a part of your life?"

Bayard's heart lurched. For a moment, he struggled to catch his breath. It was like having the wind knocked out of him. He held up a hand. "Don't, Zeph."

"Don't what?"

"Don't give me hope." His voice cracked. "I can't... I can't bear it, Zeph."

Zephyr turned to face him fully, his expression serious. "Bayard. I've watched you and Agent Thorne dance around your feelings for each other for decades. And I've watched Exandra these past few days. The way she looks at you when you're not watching? The way her face matched her hair every time Blythe Meadowsweet flattered you?" Zephyr chuckled. "I honestly thought she was going to bulldoze the barn with her fists if that overly affectionate witch touched you one more time."

"My money was on the jealous dwarves throwing the first punch." Bayard's blush only warmed his cheeks a little in the driving wind.

"That's only because you didn't see Exandra's face." Zephyr shook his head. "Merlin's beard, Bayard! Even the way she coddles Fred."

"She loves Fred—"

"She loves *you*, you daft old fool." Zephyr gripped his shoulder. "And after hearing that story, it all makes sense. I have a feeling she's just as convinced as you are that she doesn't deserve happiness. You're both so busy punishing yourselves that you can't see what everyone else sees."

Bayard stared at him, wanting desperately to believe it. "You really think...?"

"I think you should talk to her. Tell her what you just told me."

"I don't know if I can."

"Then why invite me and her on this cruise, Bay? Why'd you include us on this trip if not to find the courage to talk about the past and say the things that need to be said? You can't start this new chapter until you close out the past one."

"She's only here because of the Culture Vulture," Bayard argued. He looked away, staring out at the swirling snow.

There were icicles forming on Bayard's eyebrows. Zephyr's lips were turning blue.

"We should get back inside before we freeze solid," Bayard said. "Fred will be wondering where I am."

Zephyr looked like he wanted to say more, but he just nodded. "Think about what I said?"

"I will." Bayard turned to go, then paused. "Zeph? Thank you. For listening. For... everything."

"That's what friends are for, old man."

As Bayard opened the door back into the warmth, Zephyr called after him: "She has feelings for you, Bay. I'd stake my life on it."

Bayard didn't respond. He couldn't. The hope was almost too painful to hang onto.

A GOUDA STORY

The ship's library was tucked away on the upper deck, a cozy sanctuary of floor-to-ceiling bookshelves, plush reading chairs, and soft lamplight. A crackling fireplace dominated one wall, and frost-covered windows offered glimpses of the snow falling outside.

Wren stepped inside with Fred still in her arms, grateful for the quiet after the bustle of the atrium market. A small table near the door held the book exchange. The setup was simple. On one side of the table was a roll of brown paper, scissors, tape, assorted ribbons and trim, and markers in every color of the rainbow. On the other side of the table, a large basket was stacked with the books that had already been wrapped. Some of them were a complete mystery. Others had clues in the form of a note written on the package by the gift giver. These included hints about the genre, the types of characters found in the book, or who might enjoy reading it.

A small placard explained the simple rules for the "Blind Date with a Book."

Leave behind a wrapped book, and choose a new book of your own. We hope you will enjoy the simple magic reading.

Wren browsed the offerings, and after careful consideration, selected a slim package that seemed promising. She'd already wrapped her own contribution earlier. She was trading in a beloved travel memoir she'd read three times and was happy to pass along.

As she straightened, she nearly collided with Exandra, who'd just entered from the opposite door.

"Oh! Sorry," Wren said, juggling Fred.

"My fault entirely," Exandra replied. She held a wrapped package of her own and was eyeing the exchange table with what looked like suspicion. "I've never done this sort of thing before. Is there a strategy?"

"Just pick the one that calls to you," Wren said. "That's the fun of it. You never know exactly what you'll get."

Exandra selected a thick, square package and held it up. "Probably something terribly boring. Advanced magical theory or property law."

"And I've probably picked a bodice-ripper romance." Wren laughed. She looked at Exandra's package, then her own slim one. "Want to trade?"

Exandra blinked, surprised. "Really?"

"Why not? Yours looks more interesting."

They exchanged packages, and something about the simple, spontaneous trade made them both smile.

"Agent Thorne," Wren said, emboldened by the moment, "I wonder if I could ask you something. Would you ever consider letting me interview you? Not about the current case," she added quickly, seeing Exandra's expression shift. "But about your career. Life as an agent. I think my readers would find it fascinating."

Exandra looked like she might refuse. Then Fred quacked insistently, as if urging her to accept.

"All right," Exandra said slowly. "Why not? I'm not doing anything else productive today. Let's do it."

"Wonderful! Should we find somewhere quiet? I saw some reading nooks in the back—"

Fred suddenly launched himself from Wren's arms into Exandra's, nearly making her drop her book.

"Fred!" Wren exclaimed.

But Exandra was already cradling the duck, her whole demeanor softening. "Hello, darling boy. Have you come to keep me company?"

Fred snuggled into her arms and quacked contentedly, as if he'd found exactly where he needed to be.

"I think he's made his choice clear," Wren said with a smile. "Shall we? I think there's an alcove over by the windows."

THEY SETTLED into a small reading nook tucked into a bay window. Two wing-backed chairs faced each other across a small table, and the frosted windows created a private, cocooned feeling. Fred made himself comfortable in Exandra's lap, occasionally quacking softly as if offering commentary.

Wren pulled out her notebook. "Thank you again for doing this. My editor has been asking for more profiles of magical professionals, and—well, you're something of a legend."

Exandra snorted. "A legend. Is that what they're calling it now?"

"You've served with the Society for over eighty years. You've solved some of the most dangerous cases in modern magical history. That's impressive."

"Or stubborn." Exandra stroked Fred's feathers absently. "Depends on who you ask."

Wren carefully avoided anything classified as she asked her initial questions. She asked Exandra about joining the Society, and about what her training had been like. She was surprised by Exandra's openness. But when she probed about any particularly memorable cases, Exandra's tone cooled. She answered professionally, guardedly, the way she'd been trained to handle countless questions from civilians over the years.

As they talked, Wren noticed Exandra's gaze repeatedly drifting to a spot deeper in the library. Following her eyes, Wren saw Minerva curled up in a loveseat near the fireplace, a book laid open in her lap, looking peaceful and content.

"Minerva's quite an interesting character, isn't she?" Wren commented. "Did Zephyr speak of her much when you were at the agency together? I imagine he missed her terribly."

"I'm sure he did miss her." Exandra nodded. "But we didn't usually talk much about our lives and families back home." She thought for a moment, brow furrowing. "I supposed that her name did come up from time to time. I never understood why he insisted on staying at the Mudpuddle Bookshop every time she traveled. He said he needed to keep an eye on things there but there were others who could have done that. In retrospect, I suppose it was his way of keeping tabs on her, without things getting too complicated." Exandra sighed and Wren noticed that her eyes had gone a bit glassy.

"You worked with him for years, didn't you? He must have been an excellent partner." Wren deftly changed the subject.

"The best." Exandra's voice softened. "Zephyr was always a skilled agent. Brave, clever, dedicated. But..." She paused, watching as Zephyr himself appeared in the library, toting a teapot and two mugs.

They watched in silence as Zephyr approached his wife. Minerva had begun to doze, her chin nodding and her book slipping from her fingers. With gentle care, Zephyr set down the tea service and draped a thick shawl over her shoulders.

Minerva stirred, blinking awake, and her face transformed when she saw him. Her eyes crinkled and she beamed at him. There was no mistaking that look. It was pure joy and love.

A moment later, Minerva held up her book, flipping back a few pages to show him something on the page, and he leaned in to read it. Then she produced an iced cookie from her apron pocket. It was crumbled around the edges, but she still offered it to him. He took a bite, and it fell apart, shedding sandy crumbs into his beard.

Minerva tutted and reached up to brush them away, but she was laughing as she did it. He was laughing as well. He caught her hand and then he pulled her close and kissed her, soft and sweet and completely unselfconscious.

"That's the dream, isn't it?" Wren said wistfully.

"What is?"

"That. What they have." Wren gestured toward the couple. "Someone who knows you completely. Who makes you tea and brings you cookies and loves you even with crumbs in your beard."

Exandra's expression was complicated—wistful, sad, and something else Wren couldn't quite name. "Yes. I suppose it is."

Wren sighed, trying to picture herself eighty years from now. She could only hope she'd be half so content with her partner. And for some reason, she kept picturing Jasper. Which was ridiculous. They'd only just met.

"He seems different," Exandra suddenly volunteered, almost begrudgingly. "Zephyr, I mean. When we worked together, he was good. Professional. But he always seemed... I don't know.

Like he was holding something back. Going through the motions." She watched as Zephyr poured tea for Minerva, his movements tender. "He's not like that now. He's... present. Fully himself. Happy in a way I don't think I ever saw before."

"Do you resent it?" Wren asked gently. "That he retired and left you without a partner? That he moved on?"

Exandra was quiet for a long moment. Fred quacked softly, almost questioningly.

"I did at first," she admitted. "When Bayard gave notice so soon after Zeph left it was like... like everyone was leaving. Even the younger agents I'd trained were moving into leadership or starting families or finding lives outside the Society. And I was still there, the old war horse who didn't know when to quit."

"But you're not old," Wren protested.

"I'm one hundred and eight years old, dear. That's old by any measure." Exandra smiled wryly. "And I'm the last one left from my cohort. Everyone else found something else. Someone else. And I just keep..." She trailed off.

"Why?" Wren asked. "What's holding you there?"

The question hung in the air. Fred quacked again, more insistently this time, as if demanding an answer, too.

"I don't know how to do anything else. How to *be* anyone else." Exandra said. "I don't know who I am without the work. And I..." She swallowed hard. "I don't know if I deserve to find out."

"Why wouldn't you deserve it?"

"Because I've made mistakes. Terrible mistakes that hurt people. I—" She paused. "There are certain things I can't undo. Choices I can't take back. Maybe this is my penance. Maybe I'm meant to keep working until there's nothing left."

"That's not a life," Wren argued. "That's a prison sentence."

Fred quacked emphatically, and Exandra looked down at him.

"Don't start with me, Freddie," she said, but her voice was soft.

"He disagrees with you," Wren observed.

"He's biased. He thinks everyone deserves happiness."

Wren thought of Jasper, of the camera ornament she'd seen him sneak into his pocket. Was it meant for her? Would he have the courage to give it to her? She hoped so.

"Maybe he's right," Wren said.

Exandra shook her head. "You don't understand. When you've hurt someone...."

"Why not try riding off into the sunset anyway?" Wren posited. "I mean, what's the worst that could happen? You've got nothing to lose if you're already unhappy. You don't seem like a bad person to me. And you certainly don't seem like a coward."

Exandra frowned at her, and Wren hoped she wasn't overstepping. But one of the things she'd learned as a journalist was to ask the hard questions, and speak the truth, even when it scared you to do so. Of all the regrets people shared with her in their interviews, letting fear dictate their actions was the biggest one. Better to take the risk than to die with *what ifs*.

"Can I tell you something?" Wren said. "It's not anything to do with the article. Just an observation... person to person?"

Exandra looked up, surprised by the younger woman's boldness. "All right."

"I'm twenty-six years old. I've been a travel writer for four years now. And every single day, I'm terrified I'm not good enough. That my writing isn't special enough, my photographs aren't artistic enough, that I'm just one mediocre person in a sea of mediocrity. That I don't deserve the opportunities I've been given."

"That's not—"

"Let me finish." Wren leaned forward. "And now, suddenly there's this boy. This kind, earnest, ridiculous boy who looks at me like I hung the moon. Who I think might have bought me a perfect gift I'm not even supposed to know about yet. He makes me laugh and sees me in ways no one else does. And I've sort of been holding him at arm's length because it's the 'professional' thing to do. But that's not the real reason. The real reason is that I'm afraid. Afraid I'll disappoint him. Afraid I'm not who he thinks I am. Afraid I don't deserve that kind of love. So it just feels safer to be a little cynical."

"That's different—"

"Is it?" Wren challenged. "You made a mistake at some point. So have I! Plenty of them. The person you hurt... Do you think they'd want you to punish yourself forever?"

Exandra's pale eyes were extra bright with unshed tears. She glanced up at the ceiling and blinked a few times before answering Wren's question. "I really don't know."

"I think you do, though," Wren said gently. "And I think that's what scares you most."

Fred quacked once more, nodding his head decisively, and nuzzled himself under Exandra's chin.

In her hidden spot deeper in the library, Minerva sat very still and quiet, her book forgotten in her lap. Whether she'd wanted to eavesdrop or not was a moot point. She couldn't help it. Her mouse-enhanced hearing had caught every word of the conversation between Exandra and Wren.

It was like a scene from one of her favorite books at the Mudpuddle Bookshop and Cafe.

"What are you thinking about, my dear?" Zephyr asked, settling back beside her with his tea.

"Just listening," Minerva mused, "and thinking..."

Bayard had been searching for Fred for half an hour. After he came in from his chat with Zephyr, he'd seen the duck in the Atrium with Wren and Jasper. So he'd gone to grab a hot drink in one of the lounges and warm up. But by the time he'd returned, they were nowhere to be found.

He'd double-checked the market stalls. Fred was not hiding there. The cookie decorating station was being broken down and there was no sign of him. The staff passing out the drinks confirmed that they hadn't seen him in at least half an hour. They were pretty sure he'd left with Wren and that they'd overheard Wren saying she was headed to the library for the book exchange.

That was a problem.

Bayard had been avoiding the library because he'd caught a glimpse of purple hair headed that way earlier. His heart couldn't handle another awkward encounter with Exandra. Not yet, anyway. Not until he'd had a bit more time to process what Zephyr had said.

But Fred did love libraries and Bayard needed to find his familiar. He had no choice now. It was the last place to check.

Bayard pushed open the door. He found Wren sitting in a window nook. She wasn't writing in her notebook or interviewing anyone. She wasn't even reading. She was just sitting there, alone, staring thoughtfully at nothing.

He was surprised to see her there without Fred. She'd been so conscientious about watching him on other occasions.

"Miss Blackwood? Are you here alone? Where's Fred?"

She looked up, startled. "Oh! Yes, he's..." She pointed deeper into the library. "With Agent Thorne. She went to go do some journaling in the back alcove. I'm sorry. He just seemed to prefer her company to mine. I thought it would be okay."

Of course Fred was with Exandra.

"Of course it's okay," Bayard reassured the girl. It was not okay, however. That sneaky little duck was going to force them to interact, wasn't he?

Bayard made his way past the rows of books, stepping lightly so as not to disturb any readers. His cane barely touched the floor. He'd almost reached the alcove when he heard Exandra's voice, raw with emotion coming from the nook.

"Maybe I don't deserve to be happy, Freddie, but gods, I'm so tired of being alone."

He froze in place.

"Everyone else at the Society has moved on without me. They've all found their person, their purpose, their peace. And I'm still there, still fighting stupid battles that aren't mine to fight anymore, still pretending I'm fine when I'm —" Her voice broke. "When I'm so desperately not fine. I hate it. "

Bayard's heart cracked open. He wanted to rush in, wanted to gather her in his arms, wanted to tell her she was never alone because he'd always been right there, loving her, waiting for her.

But Fred quacked before he could move, and Exandra scrambled to her feet. She peeked around the corner.

Their eyes met.

For a long moment, neither of them moved. Exandra's face was tear-stained, vulnerable in a way he'd never seen. His own expression was equally raw, all his carefully constructed defenses shattered.

"I was just..." Bayard started. "Looking for my duck?"

"Right. It's fine. He's fine. He's right here," Exandra said quickly, wiping her eyes. She held out the exasperated looking duck. "He's been keeping me company."

"I can see that."

They stared at each other, and the air between them was electric. All the things they wanted to say, needed to say, crowded into the space but refused to emerge.

Fred quacked again, paddling his feet in the air and looking between them like he was losing patience with their ridiculousness.

"You should take him." Exandra stood abruptly. She gathered Fred under her arm and walked toward Bayard. The distance between them was simultaneously infinite and impossibly small.

She placed Fred in his arms, and their hands touched. Just for a moment. Just long enough for Bayard to feel the tremor in her fingers, the warmth of her skin, the way she didn't immediately pull away.

"Exandra," he whispered.

"Don't, Bay..." she said, but it sounded like a plea. "Please. I can't—not right now."

She stepped around him, moving quickly toward the exit. He watched her go, Fred quacking sadly in his arms.

"I know," Bayard murmured to the duck. "I know."

Across the library, Minerva and Zephyr didn't even pretend that they weren't watching the scene unfold. They knew each other too well to lie about their mutual proclivity for eavesdropping.

"They're both so miserable." Minerva sighed.

"Indeed they are." Zephyr shook his head.

"And they're both desperately in love," Minerva whispered, looking to Zephyr for a reaction.

"Indeed on that point, too." He pushed up his glasses and unfolded his newspaper, shaking it out to remove the wrinkles.

"Neither of them is going to do anything about it without *help*," Minerva continued, pushing down the newspaper with one finger. It was both a bid for attention and so she could directly look into Zephyr's eyes. Although she lacked the gift of compulsion, she wanted to be convincing.

Zephyr looked at his wife, and a slow smile spread across his face. "Uh oh. I know that look. What are you thinking, my dear?"

"I'm thinking," Minerva said, "that perhaps it's time we stopped being observers and started being a little more... proactive."

"Matchmaking, Minnie?"

"Problem-solving, Zippy. There's a difference."

He kissed her temple. "All right. Whatever you want to call it, count me in."

Minerva smiled to herself. Outside, the storm continued to rage. But inside *The Celestine Queen*, the weather was about to improve.

TO BRIE OR NOT TO BRIE

The Meaux countryside unfolded beneath *The Celestine Queen* in shades of winter green and brown. The tour group gathered in the atrium as they drifted over rolling pastures divided by old stone walls, and bare-branched trees lining country lanes. Finally, in the distance, they spied a cluster of traditional stone buildings that looked like they'd stood there for centuries.

"There," Bayard said, pointing toward the fromagerie as they passed over it. "La Maison du Lait. One of the oldest continuously operating Brie producers in France. We'll be dropping our anchor in the River Marne shortly, and proceeding by land from there."

The buildings were beautiful in their weathered simplicity. They featured typical slate roofs, thick walls, and tiny windows that Bayard explained probably dated back to the 1600s. Smoke curled from a chimney, and even from high above in the air, Minerva could even smell a hint of woodsmoke as they passed over them.

"I can't wait to try the cheese today!" Even though she was in her human form at present, Minerva could feel her whiskers twitching. That happened sometimes when she was particularly excited, as she was today. Brie cheese was her absolute favorite, and everyone in the know knew that the best Brie was from Meaux, France.

"This visit will be a little different from the others. The fromagerie we are visiting is very small and bespoke. The tour won't take us very long, but we'll be spending some more time there doing a wonderful hands-on activity that they are arranging for our group." Bayard smiled mysteriously and pressed his fingertips together, as if struggling to contain a delicious secret.

"Hands on? Is that really all you're going to tell us?" Minerva squeaked. "Should I wear anything special?"

"No need to dress any differently than you have for the other tours. Anything else you need will be provided." This was all he would say about it. He checked his pocket watch. "I'd best be going. We'll be dropping anchor very soon!"

WHEN THE SHUTTLE bus pulled into the parking lot of La Maison du Lait, two women emerged from the main building to greet them.

"Bienvenue!" called the taller of the two, a woman with short silver hair and warm brown eyes. "Welcome to La Maison du Lait. I am Margot Rousseau, and this is my wife and business partner, Claire."

Claire was smaller and rounder, with laugh lines around her eyes and flour dusting her apron. "Margot handles the cheese-making," she explained. Her English was excellent, softened by her beautiful lilting accent. "I handle everything that happens to the cheese after it's made. This includes the packaging, presentation, and all the goodness that goes on in our test kitchens. You are all in for a treat today!"

"Come, come. Let's not get ahead of ourselves. First we tour, then we create." Margot winked at her partner.

The tour group followed them into the main production building. Unlike some of the more commercial fromageries they'd visited, this one felt lived in and well loved. Broad beams crossed the ceiling overhead and the walls were decorated with a gallery of wooden rounds that documented over a century of package design. The floor was immaculate, with stones worn smooth by the centuries of feet passing over them. Bookshelves, crammed full of cookbooks and books about cheesemaking, were fitted into every spare corner. In the hallway, assorted antique tools and retired farm equipment hung from hooks on the wall or sat on display in spotlit niches like pieces of art.

"What do you suppose this thingamabob is for, Bay?" Zephyr spun the screws on a wooden framed object.

"That looks like part of a cheese press to me. Did you see this weapon over here? I'd hate to meet someone wielding one of these in a dark alley!" He pointed to the massive guillotine-like cutter on display in a glassed-in case.

Zephyr and Bayard couldn't resist tinkering with some more of the pieces, trying to guess their original purpose.

"All of these items are from our farm, and were used in cheese production right here for centuries," Margot proudly explained. She pointed out some of the more decorative metal plates and some charming figurines on a high shelf on the wall. "These are molds for shaping the cheese and those figurines were carved from dried curds, if you can believe it."

"That one looks a lot like Fred!" Wren exclaimed, pointing to a small carved duck at the end of the shelf near the door.

"That one is our mascot." Claire smiled. "You can see her in our logo as well. She brings us good luck! Shall we continue the tour?"

The first thing everyone noticed as they reached the production room was how much smaller and more intimate it was than the industrial operations they'd seen elsewhere. Wheels of Brie in various stages of ripening were set out on wooden shelves along the walls, their soft white rinds glowing softly in the morning light.

"Brie is what we call a bloomy rind cheese," Margot explained to the group. "The white coating you see is actually a mold. It's called *Penicillium candidum*. It's sprayed or dusted onto the cheese's surface, where it grows and creates that distinctive velvety rind."

"And the magic is in the mold?" someone asked.

"The magic is in everything. Not just the mold but the way it all comes together," Margot said. "The mold must grow at exactly the right rate. Not too fast, not too slow. For this to happen, the temperature must be precise. The humidity must be perfect. Too much of anything, and the rind becomes bitter or slimy. Too little, and it never develops properly."

"That does sound like some complicated spellwork," one of the passengers nodded. "I bet your family's grimoire is a big, thick one!"

"Oh, now you're speaking her language," Claire laughed.

"I'll never tell." Margot smiled mysteriously, and winked at the passenger.

GRATE MINDS THINK ALIKE

As Margot demonstrated the spraying process, Bayard and Exandra drifted toward the back of the group. They stood side by side, not quite touching, both staring at the rows of aging cheese.

"It's remarkable, when you think about it," Bayard said quietly, "how vulnerable it all is. The slightest change in humidity could ruin an entire batch."

"Mmm," Exandra agreed. "Or temperature. A few degrees off for just an hour or two, and the mold development goes wrong."

"Of course, one would have to be quite clever about it. Can't just barge in and turn off the climate controls. That would be too obvious."

"Oh, absolutely. A *theoretical* saboteur would need to be much more subtle with their gambit." Exandra's voice carried an edge. "Perhaps they could introduce a competing mold strain? Something that would look like natural contamination?" She glanced down at the ground. "Your shoe's untied. Do you want me to get that for you?"

"No. That's overly complicated," Bayard said, his tone turning critical as he set aside his cane and knelt to tie his silver laces. For a moment it was unclear whether he was referring to her theoretical plans for sabotage or her offer to tie his shoe for him. He pulled the laces tight and made a double knot while she waited. When he rose, he continued the conjecture. "Any competent cheesemaker would spot the contamination immediately. I believe a better approach would be to *slightly* adjust the humidity levels over several days. Make it look like it was an equipment malfunction."

"Your 'better approach' would take too long and leave too much evidence in the logs," Exandra scoffed. "A truly skilled operative would be more efficient. They would target the mold spraying equipment. A small mechanical failure there, and—"

"That would certainly be noticed during the next quality check. Come now, Exandra, I expected better strategic thinking from you." Bayard raked a hand through his fluffy mane.

Exandra turned to glare at him, a cold fire burning in her icy blue eyes. "Better strategic thinking? From the man who once tried to 'improve' one of my mission plans by adding seventeen unnecessary contingencies?"

"Those contingencies kept you alive!"

"Because they tied us up in meetings for six hours! That gang of undead art thieves nearly got away."

"Well, at least I think things through instead of just charging in and hoping for the best—"

"I don't charge in—"

"The Bucharest incident?"

"That was ONE time, and we needed to act fast—"

"You nearly died!" Bayard hissed. Then he stopped, noticing the beam that Exandra was about to walk into. "Watch your head."

"We didn't die in Bucharest. We were fine!" Exandra's voice had risen as she ducked her head to avoid the jutting beam. Several people turned to look at them. She lowered her voice. "And anyway, we're only talking about theoretical sabotage here. Hypothetically, if a skilled malcontent were trying to cause problems, they wouldn't use your overly cautious, take-forever approach."

"And they wouldn't use your smash-and-grab, leave-evidence-everywhere approach, either."

They glared at each other.

"Of course," Bayard said after a moment, "a *truly* clever saboteur might think outside the box entirely. Train mice to nibble only on certain molds. Or enchant the cheese to emit a frequency that disrupts the *Penicillium* growth cycle." He raised his eyebrows and cast her a sidelong glance, waiting to hear her retort. It was all he could do not to grin when she took the bait.

Exandra's lips twitched. "Train mice? That's *absurd,* Bay!"

"You have a better absurd idea, Exxie?"

"Obviously. Convince the cows to produce milk with slightly altered fat content. That changes the entire texture from the source. Nearly impossible to trace."

"Cows don't negotiate with humans," Bayard dismissed.

"Not with that attitude they don't."

"What about," Bayard said, warming to the turn of the tide in their banter, "enchanting the aging rooms to play classical music that the mold doesn't like? Studies show that bacteria are very sensitive to certain sound frequencies. Country music, for instance—"

"So your grand plan is to annoy the cheese into quitting?"

"It's theoretical!" Bayard cried.

"It's ridiculous. What about training birds to flap their wings and scatter the mold spores before they can take hold?" Exandra suggested.

"Training birds? How would they even get inside the production facility? And you criticized my mice..." Bayard snorted.

"Birds are smarter than mice."

"That is factually incorrect and you know it," Bayard argued. They'd moved even further from the group now, almost hidden behind a large aging rack.

Nearby, Minerva had positioned herself and Zephyr where they could eavesdrop without being obvious about it.

"You know," Exandra said, her voice dropping, "if we'd worked together in the field, we might have been unstoppable."

Bayard went still. "What do you mean?"

"I mean that maybe if I'd been less reckless and you'd been less cautious, we might have found a balance working together. Instead of one person charging ahead and the other person getting—" She stopped herself.

"Getting hurt?" Bayard's voice was tight. "You can say it, Exandra. Getting crippled. Getting benched. Getting relegated to desk work because I couldn't keep up."

"That's not what I—"

"Isn't it? After my accident, you went on to become one of the Society's best agents. And I became the person who answers the phone."

"That wasn't your fault. You didn't have any other choice," Exandra said, a hint of desperation in her voice. "Besides, you said you preferred research."

"What else was I supposed to say? That watching you leave for missions without me was torture? That I felt like half a man?" He laughed bitterly. "That would have been pathetic."

"It wouldn't have been—"

"Anyway," Bayard said, cutting her off, "we're discussing theoretical sabotage, aren't we? Not ancient history. There's no point in rehashing things that can't be undone, no matter how much we might wish otherwise."

Exandra looked like she'd been slapped. "Bayard—"

"Come along," he said, his voice suddenly formal. "I think Margot is about to show us where they age the cheese. We shouldn't miss it."

He walked away, leaning heavily on his cane, leaving Exandra standing alone among the cheese wheels.

Minerva watched Exandra's face crumple for just a moment before the mask slipped back into place.

"Did you hear—?" Zephyr whispered in Minerva's ear.

"Every word," Minerva confirmed. "And I think I might know how to help them."

A BRIE-UTIFUL MESS

The group had reassembled in the test kitchen toward the front of the facility. Sunlight streamed in through the windows, filtering through lacework curtains and casting frilly shadows on the countertops. Margot passed out aprons, and everyone was excited to hear more about the hands-on activity.

Minerva found herself charmed by both women, and by the clear love and partnership between them. They orbited around each other with the ease of long practice, finishing each other's sentences, sharing private smiles. Their affection was evident in almost every action. At one time, it would have made her wistful and more than a tad jealous to observe this kind of loving ease in a couple. But today, she felt differently. *They're rather like me and Zephyr*, she thought, glancing over at Zephyr. As if he'd caught her thoughts, he turned to wink at her.

All that love was clearly good for the cheese as well. The Brie from La Maison du Lait was the best she'd ever tasted.

She couldn't wait to place an order and stock some in The Squeaky Wheel.

"Today, I will be teaching you how to create the perfect Yule breakfast centerpiece with our Brie. I hope you are all ready to get your hands dirty in the most delicious way!" Claire called the group to attention. "In our family, we believe the Yule Brie should be a reflection of what you hope to bring into your life. It can be sweet or savory, simple or elaborate. That's up to you. Either way, it's a blessing you create with your own hands."

"You're teaching us how to make it?" Jasper asked, looking thrilled.

"But of course! The best way to understand Brie is to work with it. Of course..." Claire glanced back at Margot fondly. "Our cheese needs no embellishment. It is perfect as is. But everyone likes to dress up for a special occasion, so that's what my workshop will focus on today. I want to show you how to make something lovely and meaningful for your table. Welcome to my part of our realm." Claire waved a hand at the counter height workstations which had been prepped with wheels of perfectly ripened Brie, each one soft and creamy and ready to be transformed.

"For sweet preparations," she explained, "we have your choice of honey, fig preserves, fresh apples and pears, dried cranberries, pomegranate arils, pistachios, walnuts, and dates. And for more savory creations, we have mushrooms, onions, caramelized shallots, fresh herbs, garlic, prosciutto, smoked salmon, roasted red peppers, olives, and pickled vegetables."

Beside her, another table held sheets of puff pastry and premade pastry shells. Extra dough was rolled out onto chilled marble slabs. There were assorted shaped cutters in the baskets at the center.

"You can cut leaves and other shapes for decoration and I can show you how to braid the edges," Claire said. She pointed to a few examples of her elaborately trimmed and braided handiwork on the table. "This one has a raspberry filling and I used hot honey in the glaze," she explained, holding up a round that appeared to be covered in dragon scales. "Whereas this one has pickled vegetables and ham incorporated into the design and filling." The second round was decorated like a forest, with tiny pastry leaves sprouting from branches made of pickled asparagus.

"You will work in pairs," Claire continued. "Each pair should choose one wheel of Brie to create their Yule breakfast presentation. Be creative! Be bold! There is no wrong design. Think only of the blessings you wish to bring into the new year."

"All right, everyone! Find a partner!" Margot called out cheerfully and clapped her hands.

The group paired off. Minerva turned to Zephyr with a smile. Jasper's eyes found Wren's, and she nodded, moving to his side. Other passengers coupled up with friends or family members.

Bayard and Exandra, however, stood on opposite sides of the room, both studiously avoiding looking at each other.

Bayard examined the ingredient table with intense focus, as there would be a quiz later to test their knowledge of local varieties of honey. Exandra studied the ceiling beams as if she were an inspector sent to verify the building's structural integrity.

"And... that's everyone!" Claire said. "Oh, wait. There's one wheel left. Who didn't—?" She looked around. "Ah! Monsieur Fontaine and Agent Thorne. You two will share the last wheel, yes?"

Bayard's head snapped up. Exandra's gaze dropped from the ceiling to find him.

They moved slowly toward the last remaining wheel like condemned prisoners approaching the gallows.

"I suppose we'll have to be partners, then," Bayard said stiffly.

"Apparently."

They stood on opposite sides of the wheel, a good three feet between them.

"So." Bayard tapped a wooden spoon against the marble slab. "Sweet or savory?"

Exandra stared at all the scrumptious ingredients in front of her like they were alien specimens.

"I don't know. I'm not of much use in the kitchen. It's not my thing. I eat the food. I don't generally prepare it. What do you want to do?"

"I asked you first."

"I don't have a preference," Exandra said. "You choose."

"I'm fine with anything. What appeals to you?" Bayard sniffed at a bowl of chopped tarragon and wrinkled his nose. "Maybe not the tarragon, though."

"Bayard! Just pick something."

"But I want *you* to be happy with it." Bayard looked up at her with a hangdog expression. Even his bushy eyebrows drooped.

"Trolls hairbows! Honestly, I don't care. I'll be happy with whatever you choose!" Exandra rolled her eyes and flicked a bit of dough off her sleeve.

"But what if you're not? What if you're secretly craving something sweet and I choose savory?"

"Then I'll live with it!"

"But I don't want you to just 'live with it,' I want you to—" Bayard stopped himself.

"Honestly, Bay, this discussion is making me lose my appetite entirely."

Claire had appeared at their table, her expression kind. "Perhaps you two should start with the wrapping material? Would you prefer puff pastry,\ or a shell? That might help you decide the rest."

"Sure, what do you think?" Exandra asked, turning back to Bayard.

"No, what do *you* think?"

"Arrrrrghhhh!" Exandra threw her hands in the air.

"How about," Claire suggested gently, "you both gather some ingredients that appeal to you, and then see what you have? Sometimes the combination reveals itself."

She moved away, leaving Bayard and Exandra locked in a staring contest over their wheel of Brie.

Across the room, Minerva and Zephyr's table had descended into a playful argument.

"Obviously we're doing savory," Zephyr said, reaching for mushrooms. "Yule breakfast should be substantial. Filling. Something that sticks to your ribs and fortifies you for a full day of celebrating. I'm not sure about these ingredients, though. If only they'd set out some herring…"

"And stink up the whole kitchen? Herring is much too powerful to combine with Brie. Enough with your nonsense! We're doing sweet," Minerva countered, blocking his hand as he reached for the mushrooms and grabbing the honey instead. "Yule is about hope and warmth. Sweet beginnings for the new year."

"Sweet beginnings? Is that like having dessert for breakfast? What does that even mean?" Zephyr's expression was skeptical.

"It means I want honey and walnuts, you stubborn old man."

"And I want mushrooms and artichokes, you impossible woman."

They were both grinning, clearly enjoying themselves.

"How about," Minerva said, "we compromise? Half sweet, half savory?"

"You'd do that for me?" Zephyr looked surprised.

"Of course. Your happiness is more important than winning."

"But your happiness is more important than mine. Let's just do sweet."

"That's not how this works—" Minerva giggled. "You're not supposed to give in that easily."

"Isn't it? I'd gladly give up herring for the rest of my life if it meant you smiled like that every day."

Minerva's eyes went soft. "Oh, stop! You old romantic…"

"Guilty as charged." He kissed her temple. "All right, half and half it is. But I get to arrange my half."

"Deal."

At the next table, Jasper and Wren had jointly created something that looked as if it had been lifted from the set of a cooking show.

They'd carefully wrapped their Brie in strips of twisted pastry dough, creating what looked like a golden nest. Into this nest they'd arranged candied walnuts, dried cranberries, and delicate herb sprigs, and in the center—the pièce de résistance—a pastry dough version of Fred himself wearing a tiny chef's hat that Wren had fashioned from a bit of parchment.

"Fred the Call Duck is our mascot," Jasper declared solemnly. "He's the inspiration for our Yule Brie."

"Though we would never actually eat the real version," Wren said as she noted Bayard and Exandra's raised eyebrows. "He's far too precious for that."

"Should we add some pomegranate seeds?" Jasper asked. "I love the combo of red and green. So festive."

"Yes, let's do it! And maybe some of these pistachios, too?" Wren was completely absorbed in decorating their creation, her usual professional reserve gone. "Oh, and we'll need to take a picture of Fred with it before we eat it later."

"I was thinking the same." Jasper grinned. "Great minds think alike."

"FRED AS A MASCOT. I'm not sure why I didn't think of that." Bayard frowned.

Things were not going nearly as well at their station.

"Probably because it's too obvious." Exandra waved her hand at the plethora of stuffed ducks in chef hats, cheese knives with duck handles and other duck themed merch piled onto shelves near the door.

"Poor Fred. I should have brought him today. He would have enjoyed seeing this," Bayard lamented.

"He's better off on the boat. I left him with extra snacks," Exandra argued. "Though maybe he could have helped us decide on a theme for our Yule Brie."

"Peas and carrots!" they both said in unison, noting Fred's favorite snacks.

"Let's see what we've gathered," Bayard suggested, hopeful that Claire's method would save them from having to make any more painful discussion.

They laid their selections on the table.

Bayard had picked up a jar of honey, some walnuts, and a sliced pear. Exandra had collected mushrooms, garlic, and prosciutto. They now stared at the incompatible ingredients.

"Maybe we should just pick one direction," Exandra suggested.

"Fine. Which one?"

"I already said. You choose."

"And I said I want you to choose!"

"For the love of—" Exandra grabbed the puff pastry. "Fine. We're doing sweet. Are you happy now?"

"Ecstatic!" Bayard slapped the Brie on top of the puff pastry. "But we could still do savory if that's more your thing."

"I don't have a thing! I just want to get this over with!" Exandra glowered.

"Well, so do I, for the record. But you don't see me acting all miserable about it!" Bayard huffed dramatically.

"Miserable about what?" Exandra's eyes went wide.

"About being forced to partner with me. I can see why you wouldn't want to work with me in the field but is it really so awful to have to work with me in the *kitchen*?"

"I'm not miserable, I'm frustrated!" Exandra practically pounded another sheet of puff pastry on top of the cheese, stabbing it a few times with a knife before Claire rushed over, alarmed.

"Mon Dieu! I think that is enough for the venting. You do not need to murder the Brie!"

After Claire edged away, Bayard leaned in, crimping the edges of the pastry shut with a spoon.

"You're frustrated? Why? Seems like you've scored yourself a free vacation, now that we're both pretty sure there won't be any more incidents with the Culture Vulture." Bayard tipped his chin up, narrowed his eyes and leveled her with a cool, steely stare. "Why can't you just let your hair down and have a little fun with me for once?"

He was gratified to see Exandra blush a little. Her hands flew to her hair which was, in fact, already down. It was cascading to her shoulders in lovely waves and catching the sunlight . He rather liked the sparkle of the silver strands against her signature purple. And, he noticed, she was wearing lipstick. Had she always worn plum lipstick? He couldn't recall. But he liked it, so perfect on her soft, plump lips.

"You call this fun? We can't even make a simple decision about cheese without—" Exandra stopped mid sentence, breathing hard.

"Without what?" Bayard's voice was quiet.

"Nothing. Never mind. Let's just... let's do sweet and savory. You keep your honey and pears. I'm keeping the prosciutto and red onions."

They worked in tense silence, both reaching for ingredients at the same time, bumping elbows, murmuring apologies. Bayard grabbed the prosciutto and wrapped it around a slice of pear. When he laid it on top of the lumpy mound of cheese and dough it tumbled right off.

"Here, let me—" Exandra tried to help, but their hands collided and honey spilled across the workspace.

"Sorry—"

"No, my fault—"

"I wasn't watching—"

"Neither was I—"

They eventually got the Brie wrapped—sort of. Half of the pear slices were too thick, half too thin. The spilled honey had soaked into one side, making the dough look slimy. The onions on the other side refused to stay put. It looked like something an ambitious yet untalented toddler might concoct.

"It's *fine*," Exandra said, staring at their disaster.

"It's terrible." Bayard shook his head.

"Well, it's the best we could do."

"Is it? I feel like if we'd just—"

"What? Communicated better? Actually told each other what we wanted?" Exandra's voice had an edge.

Bayard flinched. "Exandra—"

"Let's just bake the cheese."

They shoved their creation into the oven, both carefully not looking at the other.

THIRTY MINUTES LATER, the smells coming from Claire's kitchen were divine. Cheese and pastry and all manner of herbs and sweetness filled the air as the cruiser proudly pulled their creations from the oven.

Claire called them to attention. "Let us see what you have created! Who would like to present first?"

Jasper and Wren shyly brought their masterpiece forward. The golden pastry nest with its perfect arrangement of ingredients was a thing of beauty, as was the toasted pastry Fred sitting atop it like a proud parent. The only issue was the paper chef's hat which had curled and discolored in the oven.

"C'est magnifique!" Claire exclaimed. "Such a beautiful presentation. I think this is art! He just needs a new hat." She handed them one of the stuffed mascots, removing the chef's hat and placing it on the pastry duck. "I think this deserves a prize. With my compliments!"

Other passengers presented their creations to similar praise. There were floral motifs and an ocean inspired round that reminded Minerva of her dear friend Hildegarde Fish back home. Minerva was proud of her and Zephyr's half-and-half Brie en croute. It came out so elegant and thoughtful, each side perfectly executed and baked. They had embellished it with a yin and yang symbol on top.

Reluctantly, Bayard and Exandra brought their creation forward.

It looked even worse coming out of the oven than it had looked going in. The pastry had puffed unevenly. One side was charred, the other pale and undercooked. The spilled honey had caramelized into dark patches like a rash. A puddle of cheese had oozed out from the stab wounds. It engulfed the sliced red onions that had landed in a soggy pink pile on the baking sheet.

"Ah," Claire said diplomatically. "An... interesting interpretation."

"We killed it," Exandra said flatly. "It's a disaster."

"Well, appearances aren't everything." Claire cut into it, releasing a cloud of steam. "Let us taste."

She took a bite, and her expression changed. "Oh, my! You know what? This is actually... quite good?"

It was true. Despite its appearance, the flavors had somehow melded beautifully. The honey and prosciutto, which shouldn't have worked together, had created a strange but delicious sweet-savory combination along with the cheese and pears. The pastry, while broken and uneven, was still perfectly flaky and buttery.

"Appearances can be deceiving." Margot beamed. "Sometimes the most delicious things come from imperfection. From two different visions finding an unexpected harmony."

Bayard and Exandra looked at each other, and for just a moment, a silent question passed between them.

But then Exandra looked away, and the moment was gone.

BACK ON *THE Celestine Queen* that evening, Minerva found Jasper and Wren seated on a sofa in the library, reviewing their photos from the day. Fred was asleep on a cushion between them, still wearing the tiny chef's hat that they'd won at the fromagerie.

Minerva thought it suited him.

"Excuse me," Minerva said. "Are the two of you terribly busy? May Zephyr and I join you for a moment?"

"Of course!" Wren looked up, concerned. "Is everything all right?"

"Everything's fine!" Minerva settled into a nearby chair, and Zephyr took the seat beside her. "Actually, we have a proposition for you. A bit of a... mission, you might call it."

Jasper and Wren exchanged wary glances.

"What kind of mission?" Jasper asked tentatively.

"The kind," Zephyr said with a slight smile, "that involves helping two very stubborn people realize they're in love with each other."

"Oh,. Wren breathed a sigh of relief. "This must be about Bayard and Exandra?"

"You've noticed, too?" Minerva asked.

"You'd have to be blind not to," Jasper admitted. "They're both so miserable and so determined not to talk about it."

"Precisely. And we think it's time someone gave them a little push." Minerva leaned forward conspiratorily. "Are you two interested in helping us orchestrate a very small, very harmless, and completely fake cheese emergency at our next stop?"

Wren's eyes lit up. "Go on... I'm listening."

"So am I," Jasper said eagerly.

"Quack!" said Fred, who was now wide awake.

Minerva smiled. "Excellent. Here's what we have in mind..."

BASKET QUESO

The next morning, Minerva, Zephyr, Wren, and Jasper sat together again, going over the scheme as they enjoyed a leisurely breakfast in the ship's dining room.

The Andalusian mountains rose before them like ancient guardians, their peaks dusted with snow that sparkled in the afternoon sun. *The Celestine Queen* floated above a valley where terraced hills cascaded down toward a ring of whitewashed buildings with terra-cotta roofs.

El Refugio de Cabra was both a working goat farm and a magical wellness retreat. It was just remote enough to keep the Ordinaries at bay, yet accessible enough to be a popular year-round destination for magical tourists in the know.

Minerva could already see goats dotting the hillsides. She counted dozens of them, their bells creating a gentle musical backdrop. Steam rose from natural hot springs hidden amongst the rocky outcroppings.

"We're all staying the night at the resort tonight?" Wren reviewed her itinerary.

"Yes, and we'll have a free day tomorrow," Jasper confirmed. "I'm looking forward to hiking, hot springs, and exploring the canyon and the gorge. Oh... there's a goat yoga session booked for us later today, too!" He frowned. "Too bad Exandra and Bayard will have to miss it."

"Goat yoga?" Zephyr raised an eyebrow. "What's this now?"

"It's a wellness activity," Jasper explained. "You do some basic yoga poses and meditate while baby goats climb all over you. Apparently it's very therapeutic."

"That's preposterous nonsense!" Zephyr snorted.

"Well, I think it sounds delightful," Minerva countered. "I love baby animals!"

A COUPLE HOURS LATER, *The Celestine Queen* dropped her anchor in a calm section of the river at the bottom of a breathtaking gorge. Sheer cliffs rose up on either side of the vessel.

"How are we supposed to get back up to the resort?" Zephyr wondered out loud as they assembled on the deck, waiting to disembark.

"Look up, dear!" Minerva elbowed him, redirecting his gaze upward to the three multicolored hot air balloons that were slowly making their way down toward the deck of the ship.

"Well, I never!" Zephyr exclaimed excitedly. He let out a low whistle. It was true. In all his many years of adventures with the Society, riding in a hot air balloon had been one of the few experiences he had missed out on.

"I've never ridden in a hot air balloon, either!" Minerva's face glowed. She was practically leaping into the air with excitement. "But I've always wanted to give it a go! What a treat to get to experience something so new and thrilling at our age, Zippy! And we get to do it together!"

"I'm glad you approve," Bayard said. "I thought it a fitting way to arrive at the resort. They do cater to adventurous travelers."

When the first balloon landed, a handsome, energetic couple hopped out from the basket. Both men wore outdoorsy-looking trekking suits that included polo shirts with the resort's logo. They were probably around forty years old, but they had a much younger air about them. Perhaps it was their obvious enthusiasm and outgoing nature as they greeted the group with warm smiles. They seemed more like beloved camp counselors excited to reunite with their favorite campers and less like resort employees who were greeting total strangers.

"¡Bienvenidos, kids!" called the taller of the two. His skin was sun-weathered and he had distinctive laugh lines around his eyes. "I'm Raoul Martinez, and this is my partner, Geraldo. Welcome to El Refugio de Cabra. Who's ready to have an awesome time?"

Geraldo was stockier and shorter, with a silver streak in his dark hair. "We are so excited to host your crew. You've come at the perfect time. Yuletide is our season here at El Refugio.

We love sharing our Queso Luna tradition with our guests from all over the world."

"Queso Luna?" a passenger asked.

"Oh, yes... The Magic Moon Cheese!" Raoul explained. "It's made from the milk of goats who graze on wild mountain herbs under the full moon. There's an old legend about it. They say the cheese has the power to reveal hidden truths and mend broken hearts."

"What kind of truths?" Wren asked, her journalist curiosity piqued.

Geraldo smiled. "The kind people carry in silence for too long. The feelings they're afraid to speak. We only eat it during the winter solstice, when the darkness is longest. The tradition says: 'what the darkness concealed, the moon's light reveals.' It gives people the courage to say what needs to be said."

"So it's like a kind of truth serum?" someone asked nervously.

"No, no." Raoul laughed. "It doesn't force anyone to speak. It simply... makes it easier. Removes the fear. Especially for those seeking to confess the love they've been afraid to confess."

"Do you believe it works?" Wren asked, her pen pausing mid sentence. She shot a look at Jasper who was suddenly preoccupied with the ropes tethering Raoul and Geraldo's balloon to the ship's deck.

"Well, I may be a bit biased," Geraldo said. "It brought us together." He and Raoul exchanged a knowing look. "But you'll have to be the judge if you try it. Just be prepared for it to be a potentially life-changing experience if you do!"

Minerva saw Bayard and Exandra exchange a quick glance, both looking away immediately.

"Enough talk. We've got so much more to share back at the resort. Who's ready to fly?"

Geraldo gestured to the waiting balloon basket, inviting the first guests in line to begin boarding.

"I think that Queso Luna sounds lovely," Minerva said, trailing Zephyr up the ramp and into the waiting balloon basket. "I just wish Zippy and I had heard about it a little sooner."

"No matter," Zephyr called out over his shoulder, his voice nearly drowned out by the roar of the burner heating the air in the balloon. He was almost as giddy about the ride as Minerva. "We're certainly making up for lost time now!"

THE BALLOONS LANDED inside a vast central courtyard surrounded by stone buildings. To the left they spied a glassed-in pavilion with steam rising from all its windows. To the right, nestled against the hillside, was the fromagerie with its distinctive round door. In the fields behind them were the stables and a barn. And straight ahead was a comfortable-looking three- story lodge with a large, outdoor communal dining area.

"You'll have the afternoon and evening to relax a bit and enjoy our facilities," Raoul said. "You can take a dip in the hot springs in the spa's bathing pavilion, and feel free to explore the meditation garden at your leisure. Tomorrow, weather permitting, will be more adventurous for those who'd like to try out some of the climbing routes in the gorge, explore a bit more in the balloons, or go mountain biking. But tonight, we'll all come together for a special dinner featuring our very own Queso Luna and other local delicacies."

As the group dispersed to get their suite assignments, Minerva noticed Bayard and Exandra carefully choosing rooms in opposite wings. They'd barely spoken to each other since the workshop disaster yesterday, both too proud and too confused to bridge the gap.

Something needed to change. And soon. Good thing the plan was already in motion. She caught Geraldo's eye and he nodded ever so subtly.

"Is everything good to go?" Wren whispered beside her. The younger woman made a show of comparing room keys with Minerva while they both pretended to study the colorful resort map.

"Yes." Minerva's cheeks were still flushed from the balloon ride. But it was the scheme that she and Zephyr had concocted that made her eyes sparkle with mischief now. "Zephyr is heading to the office with Raoul as soon as they're done with the room assignments."

She watched as Wren signaled a quick thumbs up to Jasper, who was chatting with Raoul on the other side of the lobby.

"Everything is in place." Minerva smiled. "We couldn't have pulled this off without your help. As much as I love the legend of Queso Luna, I'm worried it's going to take a little more than some full moon cheese to get those two to talk."

IN QUESO EMERGENCY

An hour later, everyone had reconvened in the courtyard for the afternoon activities. Raoul explained the goat yoga session.

"Before we tour the fromagerie, I thought you might like to meet some of our newest goats. Specifically, some of the babies in our nursery. We've planned a short session of goat yoga with them. Don't worry, they are very friendly and docile. It should be very relaxing—"

Raoul was interrupted when Geraldo suddenly burst through the door. He looked around with a concerned expression, searching for one guest in particular.

"Disculpe, Agent Thorne? There's an urgent telegram for you! It has only just arrived."

Exandra's head snapped up. "A telegram? From whom?"

"The Society for the Protection of Natural Magic, it says. It seemed important, so I brought it out to you, rapido!"

Exandra took the envelope, her brow furrowing. She opened it and scanned the message, her face growing paler by the moment.

"What is it?" Bayard asked, moving closer.

"It's from headquarters." Exandra's voice was tight. "Apparently the Culture Vulture has struck three new locations overnight. Two in France, one in Germany. All facilities known for producing popular Yuletime cheeses. They say they're concerned this is an even more well coordinated attack than they thought at first and—" She paused, reading the second half of the message. "They want me to check in for an urgent call from the director." She turned to Geraldo. "I'm sorry. Is there a secure line where I can take a call privately?"

"A private call?" Raoul looked appropriately concerned. "Of course, yes. Geraldo can show you down into the fromagerie. We have a conference room just inside the cheese caves. Very secure. It has excellent reception and complete privacy."

"Thank you." Exandra turned to address the group. "You all should continue on with the activities without me. There's no need for everyone to be disrupted. Please rest assured that I'm on the case and I'll rejoin you as soon as I can."

"I'm coming with you," Bayard announced. He held out Fred's carrier toward Wren. "Would you—?"

Wren took the carrier before he finished the sentence.

"Bayard, that's not necess—" Exandra began to object.

"This is my tour group and this is my responsibility. And, if the Culture Vulture's activities are escalating, you might need backup. Besides, two sets of eyes are better than one if there's any reconnaissance needed." He gripped his cane. "I still have agent-level clearance, and I'm not letting you face this criminal alone."

Exandra hesitated. Then something like gratitude flickered in her expression. "All right, then. Come along if you must." She paused again before adding, "Thank you, Bay."

Geraldo led them away from the group. Behind them, Minerva exchanged a significant look with Zephyr, who gave the tiniest wink.

"Well, then!" Raoul said brightly. "Everyone else, let's proceed to the meadow for some goat yoga. I promise it will be an experience you won't forget!"

DUCK, DUCK... GOAT

The meadow was perfect. There was soft grass and glorious mountain views. They were greeted by a rainbow-colored palette of yoga mats arranged in a circle. But the group barely noticed the scenery or the artistic arrangement of the mats. They were far too focused on the pen full of the most adorable, tiny, fluffy baby goats waiting to play with them.

"Oh, my goodness! They're so small!" Wren exclaimed, already pulling out her camera.

"Eight weeks old," Raoul confirmed. "Very playful, very curious. They'll climb on you, nibble your clothes, and generally be delightful distractions while you attempt to find inner peace. But on the other hand, they are excellent helpers. They force us to remain present when the mind begins to wander."

Fred, who Wren had only just let out of his carrier, took one look at the goats and quacked indignantly. He positioned himself between Wren and the small goats, spreading his wings protectively and squawking louder.

"Fred, it's okay," Wren said, trying not to laugh. "They're just babies. They're just curious about us."

Fred was having none of it. Every time a goat approached, he intercepted, herding it away with aggressive quacking and wing-flapping.

"Uh oh, I think he's jealous," Jasper observed from where he was settling onto a green yoga mat. He bit back a laugh as a small white goat jumped onto his lap and nibbled at his chin.

"Fred is most definitely jealous," Raoul agreed, amused. He turned back to Wren and shrugged. "I'm sorry. Perhaps it will have to be duck yoga instead of goat yoga for you?"

"Seems I don't have any other choice," Wren said, looking wistfully back at the goats.

And so, while everyone else attempted to meditate with baby goats climbing all over them, Wren sat cross-legged with Fred perched contentedly on her shoulder.

"That's it." Raoul led them through a series of simple poses. "Just try and stay present in the moment. Let the goats do their thing. And breathe!"

Jasper had just settled into child's pose when a small brown goat decided his back was the perfect napping spot. The goat curled up, closed its eyes, and fell asleep.

"Um," Jasper said, "I think I'm stuck."

"Don't move," Wren whispered, quickly pulling out her

camera from the bag beside her and snapping some photos. "This is too adorable."

Zephyr, attempting corpse pose with a ginger-colored baby ewe, found himself so relaxed by the mountain air and gentle afternoon sun that soon he was snoring as well, the baby goat nestled against his side.

Minerva, holding her own in tree pose, looked over at her sleeping husband, at Fred's protective stance over Wren, and at Jasper pinned by his napping goat, and smiled. She'd been so nervous to leave Primrose Court for the holidays but she needn't have fretted so much.

Her Yuletime vacation was turning out even better than she'd dared to imagine. This was exactly the kind of peaceful chaos she'd hoped for on this trip.

Now, if only the chaos they'd planned in the cheese caves would work out as well.

WORST QUESO SCENARIO

Geraldo led Bayard and Exandra through the fromagerie. When they reached the back, he opened a door that led down a stone staircase into the cheese caves. The temperature dropped precipitously, and the air filled with the earthy smell of aging cheese and damp stone.

"The conference room is here at the back," Geraldo explained. "We use it sometimes for private tastings and business meetings. It's very quiet, very secure."

They wound through narrow passages lined with wooden crates, going deeper into the mountain. Finally, Geraldo stopped in front of a heavy wooden door. Through a small window, they could see a desk with a telephone on it.

"Here we are. It's unlocked. The phone is hardwired directly to the main house. The call should come through any moment. Can I bring you anything while you wait? Water? Coffee?"

"No, thank you. I'm fine," Exandra said. She wrung her hands and bit her lip, clearly anxious about this call.

"I'll be fine as well." Bayard waved off the offer. "This shouldn't take too long."

Geraldo nodded and turned to go. His footsteps echoed back up the passage as he left.

The space behind the door seemed a bit small to call it a conference room. It was windowless, carved directly into the rock. A wooden desk sat against one wall. There was nothing on the desk besides an old-fashioned rotary telephone. There was also a round table with four chairs. A filing cabinet. And along the walls, more wheels of cheese, each one marked with strange symbols and numbers.

"Well," Bayard said, taking a seat. "I suppose that now we just wait for that call."

They sat in uncomfortable silence. After a few moments, Bayard stood up to examine the cheese wheels. Exandra paced. Five more minutes passed. Then ten.

"How long does it take to place a call?" Exandra muttered.

"Maybe there's a delay—"

Suddenly a series of red lights began flashing in the corners of the room. And then they heard a spine-tingling scream.

"What the—?" Exandra moved toward the door.

It was locked.

"Bayard, the door won't open!"

He tried it himself. She was right. Solid. Sealed tight. The scream repeated. The exact same scream.

"Is that even a human being?" Exandra cocked her head.

"I'm not sure... It's coming from the speakers in the ceiling," Bayard observed.

By the third time, the scream was not so much alarming as annoying.

"I wish there was a way to turn that off." Exandra frowned.

"You know, I think it's actually a goat," Bayard posited. "You've heard of screaming goats?"

"I'm not sure I can unhear them." Exandra stuck her fingers in her ears as the screaming goat bleated for a fourth time.

The telephone on the desk rang. Exandra grabbed it.

"This is Agent Thorne—"

A recorded message played, the voice tinny and artificial:

"This is a recorded message. The Emergency Response Protocol has been activated. Temperatures are rising in the storage sector due to the unaddressed buildup of pressure in the neighboring hot springs. The cheese cultures are in danger of catastrophic contamination. Sixty minutes till meltdown."

The line went dead.

"I hear footsteps!" Bayard exclaimed, his ear pressed against the door. He rapped against it with his cane. "Hello? Geraldo! Can you please let us out? There seems to be some kind of emergency happening and we've been locked in!"

"Try your wand?" Exandra suggested.

"Excellent idea!" Bayard reached into his pocket and pulled out his trusty wand. He waved it at the locked door.

Nothing happened.

"Sera solvo!" He tried again, this time using the Latin spell for unlocking doors.

Still nothing.

"Desbloquear!" He tried a third time in Latin. But the lock would not budge. "The door must be warded." He sighed.

Suddenly, a folded piece of paper shot under the door and skittered across the smooth stone floor.

Exandra bent to retrieve it and unfolded it. She read the message aloud.

"Solve the puzzles to access the emergency controls." Her eyes widened. "It's signed, 'The Culture Vulture' and there's a P.S. It says, 'good luck."

Bayard sat down at the desk. He picked up the phone and held the receiver to his ear. Then he pressed the receiver back down and picked it up again. He checked the cord. "There's no dial tone. I don't think this line is working."

Exandra continued to stare down at the note. "Bayard, you don't think this is really—"

The screeching interrupted them again, causing them both to jump.

"I don't know what to think. I can hardly think at all, what with that stupid screaming goat!" Bayard snapped. "Silencio!" He pointed his wand at the speaker.

With a crackle, the alarm went silent. A moment later, the sounds of the screaming goats were replaced with elevator music.

"Are you kidding me?" Exandra groused at the speakers. Then the overhead lights buzzed for an instant and a digital clock on the wall flickered to life, beginning a countdown sequence: 60:00. Then 59:59. 59:58.

"Oh, good gracious gods," Bayard breathed. "I'm not sure how or why this is happening, but it would appear that the threat to the facility is real. Someone must have targeted the facility for sabotage before we arrived. That's why the telegram—to get us out of the way."

"While they trap us here in some sick kind of game of cat and mouse," Exandra finished.

"Don't you mean cheese and mouse?" Bayard laughed bitterly.

"Bayard, that isn't funny!" Exandra pursed her lips.

"Do you think we might have manifested this, Exxie? He glanced down worriedly at his wand. "What if all of our crazy machinations summoned a real-life Culture Vulture?"

"You know as well as I do that's not likely, Bay. Neither of us has ever wished any real harm on the Yule cheeses."

"Yet here we are." Bayard gestured to the clock.

57:17 remaining.

"Okay, Bayard." Exandra's face became a mask of calm as she slipped into professional mode. "Here are the facts. If the hot springs pressure breaches the caves and makes the temperature rise too high, the cultures will become contaminated and you know what that means..."

Bayard finished her thought.

"No Queso Luna for the Yule celebration. No midnight revelations and shared joy for the villagers. Exactly what someone like the Culture Vulture wants!"

They stared at each other, fear and determination mixing.

"We're not going to let that happen," Bayard said, rising to his feet again.

"We need to solve these puzzles," Exandra said. "Fast."

THE FIRST PUZZLE revealed itself immediately: a section of the wall slid aside, revealing a message chalked into the stone:

ONLY STRENGTH CAN MOVE WHAT TIME HAS SET. FIND THE MARKED WHEELS AND PLACE THEM IN ORDER OF AGE.

Exandra looked around. Four massive cheese wheels sat on a platform, each easily fifty pounds. Above them, four empty shelves were each marked with a year: 1847, 1923, 1965, 2001.

"The wheels must have the dates somewhere," Bayard said, moving closer. "But they're on the bottom. We have to lift them to see."

Exandra cracked her knuckles. "That, I can do."

She lifted the first wheel—heavy even for her considerable strength—and turned it so Bayard could see the carved date on the bottom.

"1965!"

She placed it on the corresponding shelf. Then the next: 2001. Then 1923. Finally, 1847.

A grinding sound, and a door opened in the far wall.

55:27 remaining.

They rushed through into the next chamber. This one was filled with bottles of various liquids, each labeled with handwritten specimen labels with Latin inscriptions. A whiteboard on the wall displayed a question:

WHICH THREE CULTURES ARE REQUIRED FOR AUTHENTIC QUESO LUNA? SELECT CORRECTLY OR PREPARE FOR THE MELTDOWN.

"This is your specialty," Exandra said. She held up her hands. "It's all you."

Bayard studied the bottles, his mind racing. Queso Luna. Fresh goat cheese. What cultures would they use?

"*Lactococcus lactis,*" he murmured. "Definitely. And *Leuconostoc mesenteroides* for the texture. And..." He examined the other options. "*Lactobacillus rhamnosus.* Those three."

He selected the bottles and placed them on the tray on the counter. They waited a moment, Bayard afraid he'd chosen wrong.

Another grinding sound. Another door.

49:23 remaining.

The third chamber contained what looked like a large wooden cutting board mounted on the wall, its surface covered in carved symbols and patterns. Cheese wheels marked with matching symbols sat on a nearby table.

DECODE THE PATTERN. PLACE THE WHEELS IN THE CORRECT SEQUENCE TO CLEAR THE PATH FORWARD.

"It's a cipher," Bayard said, excitement cutting through his fear. "Look here: These symbols correspond to traditional cheesemaking marks. Each one represents a stage of production."

"Can you read it?" Exandra asked.

"I think so. This one—" He pointed to a symbol. "—represents the curdling stage. And this one is pressing. This is aging. This is..." He worked through the logic, his fingers tracing the patterns. "They need to be arranged in the order of production. Curdling, cutting, pressing, salting, aging, wrapping."

They worked together, Exandra lifting the heavy wheels while Bayard directed placement. When the final wheel clicked into place, a hidden panel slid aside, revealing a narrow passage.

42:15 remaining.

"Through here," Exandra said.

But the dimly lit passage was more than simply narrow. It was an agility course that wound them up through the aging caves. Low ceilings, tight turns, places where they had to squeeze between the racks. The final section required climbing back down a ladder while maintaining three points of contact.

"I'll go first," Exandra said. She wanted to be somewhere she could catch him if he fell. She could never forgive herself if he got hurt again.

"No, I will." Bayard moved toward the entrance.

"Bayard, with your leg—"

"My leg is fine."

"It's not fine, and this requires agility—"

"I'm not helpless, Exandra!"

"I never said you were!"

"Didn't you?" His voice cracked. "Isn't that what you've thought about me for the past eighty years? That I'm broken? Damaged? Someone who needs to be protected and left behind?"

"That's not—" Exandra's eyes filled with tears. "Bayard, no. That's not what I think at all."

"Then leave me alone and let me do this." He stopped, breathing hard. "Please."

They'd navigated the course together. Bayard's limp had made certain moves difficult, and twice Exandra had braced him when his cane slipped. But he hadn't complained or hesitated in asking for help when it was necessary. She stared at him, forcing herself to stand down. "All right, Bay. I'm right behind you."

But she still couldn't make herself watch while he climbed down. She closed her eyes and held her breath till she heard him shout up to her. Then she quickly climbed down after him.

At the bottom of the ladder, they found themselves in a larger chamber with a control panel on the wall. A heavy metal door marked with a lit "Exit" sign stood before them, still locked.

FINAL CHALLENGE: ENTER THE SEQUENCE TO RESTORE TEMPERATURE CONTROL AND PREVENT CONTAMINA-TION. USE EVERYTHING YOU'VE LEARNED.

The digital panel displayed a series of spaces waiting to be filled in. The keyboard was rife with possibilities. Numbers, letters, symbols. The "sequence" was an elaborate password of sorts. It could be anything. Exandra leaned against the cold stone wall, resisting the urge to pull her hair out.

"How will we ever figure out what numbers to choose?" she moaned.

"I think it's all of them," Bayard mumbled as he realized. "The years from the wheels. The cultures we selected. The cipher pattern. We have to combine them in the right order."

3:42 remaining.

"The years were 1847, 1923, 1965, 2001," Exandra recalled. "And the cultures—"

"*Lactococcus lactis, Leuconostoc mesenteroides, Lactobacillus rhamnosus.*"

"And the cipher sequence—curdling, cutting, pressing, salting, aging, wrapping."

They stared at the panel, trying to see the pattern.

2:15 remaining.

"Wait," Bayard said. "The symbols—they corresponded to years. Each stage of cheesemaking has a traditional time period. If we match them—"

His fingers flew over the panel, entering the combination: dates, culture abbreviations, symbols in sequence.

0:47 remaining.

"That's not working," Exandra said, her voice tight.

"Try reversing it," Bayard suggested. "Newest to oldest?"

Exandra's large, agile hands flew across the panel.

0:23 remaining.

At the very last moment, a green light flashed.

The door clicked open.

They stood there, breathing hard, covered in dust and sweat, and for a moment, they just looked at each other. Then they embraced. But only for a moment.

"We did it," Exandra whispered.

"We did."

They stumbled through the door, back into the open air. They were standing in a private patio off the side of the fromagerie. And what they found there made both of them gasp.

AT A LOSS FOR CURDS

The sun was setting but the tile beneath their feet was still warm from the afternoon sunshine. Two outdoor spaceheaters, twin pillars of lit flame, would continue to keep the space warm for hours. It was a private setting; the thick vines that grew on the trellis walls provided a barrier, sheltering the patio from the rest of the courtyard's view. Candles covered every spare surface, their light reflecting off the stone walls. It was the perfect setting for a romantic alfresco dinner, and the scene was set for precisely that.

A small table sat in the center of the space, draped in white linen, set for two diners. Wine glasses. Fresh flowers. And in the center of the table, a perfect wheel of Queso Luna, topped with blue orchids. It was already sliced and arranged on a board alongside some bread, olive tapenade, and sliced fresh fruit.

Soft music played from somewhere. Bayard recognized something classical and nauseatingly romantic.

And standing beside the table, looking entirely too pleased with themselves, were Minerva and Zephyr. They were clapping.

Clapping.

"Congratulations!" Minerva said warmly. "You two did it! You escaped with time to spare."

Bayard stared. "What the devil—?"

"The escape room!" Zephyr exclaimed. "Quite clever, wasn't it? Raoul and Geraldo designed it for team-building exercises. We thought it would be perfect for—"

"Wait a minute..." Exandra's voice was dangerously low and quiet. "The *escape room?*"

"The telegram was fake?" Bayard asked, his face going pale. "The emergency? The countdown?"

"The whole thing?" Exandra gasped.

"All part of the game," Minerva said. "Though you took it wonderfully seriously. Really committed to the—"

"You—" Exandra's hands clenched into fists at her side. "You tricked us and you trapped us. You faked an emergency. You made us think—" Her voice rose. "Do you have any idea how worried we were? We thought the entire facility was going to be destroyed! We thought—"

"We thought people would be hurt," Bayard added, his voice shaking. "We thought the Culture Vulture's efforts to destroy Yuletime celebrations had escalated. We thought —" He had to sit down. Once seated, he looked up at Minerva, anger and betrayal written across his face. "How could you two?"

Minerva and Zephyr exchanged a nervous look. This was not exactly going how they'd imagined it would.

"We were only trying to help," Minerva squeaked. "You two have been dancing around each other for days, for decades, and neither of you will just talk—"

"So you manipulated us?" Exandra's voice boomed. "Locked us up in a room together? Thought you'd force us into some sort of—of—" Her lip curled as she gestured at the romantic setup. "This?"

"Well, yes," Zephyr said, stepping in front of Minerva protectively. "That was rather the point, Exxie. It's not like either of you were going to listen to reason. You needed a good shake-up, if you ask me!"

"Well, we didn't ask you!" Bayard objected.

"Didn't you?" Zephyr's brow raised. "I seem to remember chatting with you on the frozen deck—"

"That still didn't give you the right to do this!" Bayard growled. His hands shook as he gripped his cane and stood back up. "Poorly done, you two!"

He turned and stormed away, his cane thwacking sharply against the stone floor.

"Bayard, please! Wait—" Minerva started to follow.

"Oh, no, you don't! You leave him alone," Exandra snapped, glowering at Minerva as she blocked her path. "You're going to leave us both alone. You've done enough for one day."

With this, she stomped off in the opposite direction, her footsteps echoing through the courtyard.

Minerva and Zephyr stood alone in the candlelit chamber, surrounded by their carefully planned romantic setup.

"Well," Zephyr said after a long moment. "That did not go quite like we hoped it would, did it?"

"No," Minerva agreed softly. "No, it didn't." She hated to admit it, but maybe they shouldn't have meddled. "Maybe we shouldn't have..." she said sadly.

They looked at each other, then at the beautiful dinner they'd arranged. The tapas smelled delicious.

"Think we should go after them?" Zephyr asked.

"I don't think they'd welcome that right now." Minerva sighed. "I think in our desire for our friends to be as happy as we are, we pushed too hard, too fast, Zippy."

"Maybe we should have waited until after they ate the Queso Luna cheese." Zephyr heaved a sigh. "So what should we do now?"

Minerva looked at the table, at the wine and cheese and candles. It would be a shame to let it all go to waste.

"I think we need to let them be and we have some dinner," she said. "We give them space. And tomorrow, we'll have to apologize."

They sat down at the table meant for two other people, and Zephyr poured the wine.

Minerva bit into her slice of Queso Luna, enjoying how it was both sharp and creamy at once and how it made her tongue tingle.

"Do you think they'll forgive us eventually?" he asked.

"I hope so," she said. "And I hope they find a way to get over themselves, too. Because they really need each other. Even if they don't know it yet. Just like we needed each other. And Zippy?"

Zephyr bit into his slice of cheese and made a "mmmmm?" sound.

For a moment, the two of them just stared into each other's eyes.

"I know, Minnie. I love you, too. Always have, always will. "

COME TO CHEESES

Bayard hadn't slept a wink.

He'd tried. He'd lain in his comfortable bed at El Refugio de Cabra. The pillows were fluffy down, and the duvet a silky cotton. And yet he could not quiet his mind. He'd listened to the night sounds of the mountains. The wind whistled through pine trees and he could hear the distant bells of goats. The ever-present whisper of the hot springs hissed and bubbled beneath all those other sounds. Fred had curled up beside him, occasionally quacking softly in his sleep and flapping his feet as if to paddle, but Bayard had just stared at the ceiling, replaying the entire evening over and over.

The escape room. The worry for their new friends and all the cheesemakers. As far-fetched as it now seemed, playing it back in his mind, they'd both been convinced the threat from the Culture Vulture was real. Perhaps that was because they'd wanted to believe it. To have something to fight for, together. He replayed the moment the light turned green over and over in his head. He had a hard time savoring their relief when they finally solved the puzzles.

Because then there was that moment immediately after, when they realized they'd walked into a set-up.

The ridiculously romantic dinner. The candles. Minerva and Zephyr's smug faces.

Well—perhaps they weren't smug so much as *pleased*. Pleased with themselves? Or pleased for him and Exandra? He wasn't sure what the difference was, but he supposed it was also the difference between betrayal and misguided meddling.

Regardless, he'd felt so manipulated. So foolish. Like a puppet whose strings had been yanked. They had overstepped.

But, if he was being honest with himself, underneath the anger and embarrassment was something else. Something he couldn't quite name.

He couldn't stop thinking about the vulnerability on Exandra's face when she'd realized they were trapped. She'd turned to him for guidance. And the way she'd looked at him when he'd done just fine, navigating the agility course despite his limp. And yes, even the way she'd embraced him just before that final moment when they'd tumbled through the last door together, panting, having just saved (they'd thought) an entire facility.

Working together had been amazing. Even if it was only for an hour. Even if it was totally fake. When push came to shove, they'd made pretty good partners.

He gave up on sleep around five in the morning, dressed, slipped into his trainers, and stepped out into the pre-dawn darkness.

The courtyard was empty, lit only by a few lanterns and the stars overhead. Frost glimmered on the stone pathways. Bayard walked slowly, his cane grazing the stones beside the path. He was following no particular route. Just moving because staying still was impossible.

He rounded a corner near the spa facility and meditation gardens and stopped in his tracks.

Across the courtyard, silhouetted against the steam rising from the heated water in the pool, stood Exandra.

She wore her bathing suit and appeared to be warming up for a swim. She performed a series of arms circles, then swung her arms from side to side, rotating her shoulders and wrapping her arms around herself. She wore a black and gold swimsuit, and her hair was tucked back into a matching gold swimcap. Without her hair to soften and hide the lines of her face, and clothes to hide the natural curves and strength of her body, he thought she looked even more beautiful, if that were possible. Her strong, proud features were larger than life. With her broad shoulders and generously curvy figure, Exandra looked like a statue of one of the old gods, come to life.

But she didn't look happy. Even from this distance, he could see the tension in her stance, the way she kept shaking her head like she was arguing with herself.

He should go back. Give her space. They'd both said they wanted to be left alone.

But his feet wouldn't move.

She turned, still stretching, and saw him outside.

They froze, staring at each other through the glass.

For a long moment, neither moved. Then Exandra looked away, raised her arms in the air, and dove into the pool so gracefully, she barely made a splash.

Bayard watched her swimming away from him, something in his chest aching so fiercely he had to press his hand against it.

They were both awake. Both alone in the darkness. Both too proud or too scared to close the distance between them.

He turned and walked the other way, and if his vision blurred a little, he told himself it was just the cold mountain air making him tear up.

By eight o'clock, the lodge's dining room had filled with passengers enjoying a leisurely breakfast at the buffet. The smell of fresh pastries and coffee competed with the mountain air streaming through open windows.

Bayard sat alone at a corner table, pushing his frittata around his plate without eating. Fred pecked at a bowl of fruit beside him, occasionally quacking at him with what sounded like concern.

"Nonsense. I'm absolutely fine, Fred," Bayard reassured the duck. "Just tired."

"Liar," said a familiar deep voice.

Bayard looked up to find Minerva and Zephyr standing beside his table, their expressions serious.

"May we sit?" Minerva asked gently, but she clearly wasn't taking no for an answer. She was already pulling out a chair.

"I'd rather be alone—" Bayard sniffed.

"Too bad," Zephyr said, settling into the chair on his other side. "We need to talk to you."

Across the room, Exandra had just emerged from the buffet, carrying a plate of food. She was moving warily toward the tables. She took one look at the trio at Bayard's table, froze, and pivoted toward the opposite corner.

"Agent Thorne!" Minerva called out loud enough for the request to be impossible to ignore. "Please join us."

Exandra's shoulders stiffened. She held up a finger. For a moment, Bayard thought she might refuse. But then she grabbed herself a mug of coffee and stalked over to their table, sitting as far from everyone else as possible.

"What do you want now?" she asked, her voice flat.

"To apologize," Minerva said simply. "Last night was... a bit over the top. I'll admit it. We pushed too hard. We stressed you both out, and that wasn't fair of us."

"Dying dragon's breath right, it wasn't fair!" Exandra's voice was low but nostrils flared as she lightly pounded the table with one fist.

"However," Zephyr continued, "we're not sorry for the general premise. You two really needed to talk. I'm guessing you still do. Actually talk. Not dance around each other, not make excuses, not pretend everything's fine when you're both clearly miserable."

"We're not—" Bayard started.

"You look like you haven't slept," Minerva said gently, looking at him. "You've been awake since—what? Three? Four in the morning?"

Bayard's silence was answer enough.

"And you," Zephyr said, turning to Exandra. "You've been pacing the grounds since dawn. Don't think I didn't see you from our window."

Exandra glared into her coffee.

"Look," Minerva said, "we know this isn't easy. Transitions never are, especially when there are so many years of history and hurt between you. But Zephyr and I—we didn't just slide into our happy ending, either."

Bayard looked up, surprised. "What do you mean? You two found each other again and everything just... worked."

"Oh, is that what happened?" Zephyr raised an eyebrow. "Minnie, did everything *just work* when we reconnected?"

"Certainly," Minerva said dryly. "If by 'worked,' you mean I got stuck in mouse form in a disapparated house with no way to communicate who or where I was, and you nearly died in an extended coma from a true love's kiss hex, then yes. It all went swimmingly."

Bayard blinked. "I... I didn't realize..."

"That's because you weren't there," Minerva said. "You heard the happy ending version. Two childhood sweethearts reunited after decades apart, living happily ever after at their fromagerie. But the actual process was messy and terrifying and required both of us to be extraordinarily vulnerable and brave."

"We almost lost each other multiple times," Zephyr added. "Because we were both so scared of being hurt again. So scared of admitting what we felt for each other."

Exandra was staring at her coffee like it held the secrets of the universe. "That's different," she argued. "You two had a first time. A childhood romance. Something real to build on. We never really—" She stopped herself.

"Never what?" Minerva asked gently.

"Nothing. It doesn't matter."

"It clearly does matter," Zephyr said. "Bay, Exandra—we also know something else. Something we probably should have confronted you about earlier instead of trying to engineer a romantic revelation."

Bayard went very still. "What do you mean?"

Minerva took a breath. "We know you've both been sabotaging the cheese production. There's no Culture Vulture."

The silence that followed made their ears throb.

Fred quacked nervously.

"I...ummm... don't have any idea what you're talking about," Exandra said, but her voice lacked conviction.

"Don't," Minerva said firmly. "We overheard your 'theoretical sabotage' discussion. We've watched you both acting guilty and confused. We've noticed that every incident has coincidentally occurred when one or both of you were not present and accounted for."

"Not to mention the fact that the 'trouble upstream' someone named 'Mayard Pontaine' phoned in was complete and utter nonsense." Zephyr chuckled. "I pulled a few strings and read the report. 'Suspicious loitering near cheesemaking facilities' is hardly the stuff the Society normally sends its top agents to investigate." Zephyr did his best impression of a headmaster, raising his eyebrows and looking down his nose, first at Bayard and then at Exandra.

Bayard's face was burning. "Zephry... Minerva..."

"We're not judging you," Zephyr interrupted. Then he bit back a smile. "Okay. Well, maybe I'm judging a little. *Mayard Pontaine?* Really? The point is, you *both* did this. You both have kept this whole ridiculous Culture Vulture scenario alive because you were desperate to stay near each other. And now you're both too stubborn and too scared to just admit it and talk about why you did it."

"So here's what's going to happen," Minerva said. "You're going to talk to each other. Really talk. Figure out what you want. Because we can't keep locking you in rooms together—"

"You'd better not," Exandra rumbled.

"—but we also can't watch you both be this miserable when the solution is sitting right across the table from you."

"I don't know if I can," Exandra whispered.

"Why not?" Zephyr asked.

"Because it's not that simple. We're not—" She gestured helplessly. "We're not like you two. We don't have that easy comfort, that natural partnership. We have a history of being bad for each other. Of hurting each other. We're just—"

"Broken," Bayard finished. "We're just broken. Or maybe it's just me."

"You're not broken," Minerva said firmly. "You're scared. There's a difference."

She stood up, and Zephyr did the same. "We're leaving now. You two can sit here and talk, or you can continue avoiding each other and being miserable. Your choice. But Bayard? I noticed you signed up for the canyoning group that's hiking down into the gorge this morning?"

"I did," Bayard confirmed.

Exandra's head snapped up. "You *what*?"

"Maybe," Minerva continued, ignoring Exandra's reaction, "you could both go and use that time to have a real conversation. Away from everything else. Just the two of you."

Bayard looked out the window, and Exandra stared at her hands, both stubbornly refusing to respond.

"Okay then. This duck needs a proper breakfast, by the way, not just a bowl of fruit." Minerva pushed her chair back in and held out an arm for Fred. He hopped right onto it, approval for this plan radiating from his beady little eyes. "And you two need privacy."

They left, taking Fred with them.

Bayard and Exandra sat silent and alone at the table, not quite looking at each other, the weight of everything unsaid pressing down on them both.

THE G.O.A.T

"Canyoning!" Exandra exclaimed. "Of all the activities on offer, you signed up for *canyoning*."

"Yes. Yes I did."

"In a *gorge*."

"That's generally where activities like canyoning take place."

"Bayard." She turned to face him fully, and he could see the fear in her eyes. "You can't. Not with your leg. Not in water. Not in a gorge, of all places—"

"My leg is fine, Exandra. It hasn't given me any trouble in years."

"It's not fine! You have a limp, you use a cane, and you're talking about rappelling down waterfalls and climbing over rocks and—" Her voice broke. "You might get hurt."

"Or, I might surprise you," Bayard countered. "I'm very fit for my age and a great deal more capable than you think.

Just because I use a cane and walk with a limp doesn't mean I'm not able to do those sorts of things. I just might do them a little more slowly."

"I know you're capable of doing all kinds of things. You certainly demonstrated that yesterday. But this seems reckless. This is—" She stopped, pressing her hands to her face. "Have you even been canyoning since the accident?"

"I have not," Bayard confessed.

"Then why? Why would you do this now?"

"Because I need to," he said simply. "Because ninety years ago, I had an accident in a gorge, and I've been afraid of them ever since. And I'm tired of being afraid. I'm tired of letting that one moment dictate everything I can and can't do."

"Bayard—"

"And maybe," he continued, his voice hardening, "I'm tired of you thinking I need to be protected. That I'm so fragile. That I can't handle myself."

"That's not what I think!"

"Isn't it?" He stood up, gripping his cane. "You've spent ninety years treating me like I'm made of glass. And I let you, because I thought that's what you needed. To feel like you were protecting me. Making up for—" He stopped himself.

"Making up for destroying your career?" Exandra's voice was sharp. "For crippling you? For taking away everything you should have been?"

"For something that wasn't even your fault!" The words burst out of him. "For an accident that I caused by ME being reckless and stupid and trying to impress you!"

They stared at each other, breathing hard.

"I'm going canyoning." Bayard's left eye twitched. His jaw was set. "I'm facing this. And you can either come with me, or you can stay here. But I'm done playing it safe and hiding from things that scare me."

He walked away, his cane smacking the floor with frustrated self-loathing thwacks. Technically, he'd just told another lie. If he was really done hiding, he would have stayed planted in his seat and told her that even after all these years, he was still in love with her.

Exandra sat alone at the table for several minutes, her hands shaking.

Then she stood and marched herself into the activities office. She was going to speak with Geraldo and get herself added to the canyoning group.

THE CANYONING GROUP WAS SMALL. There were only six people total including Bayard and Exandra, plus their guide, a weathered Andalusian man named Carlos who'd been running groups through these gorges for forty years.

"The water is a little higher than normal today," Carlos explained as they geared up. "Recent rain in the mountains.

Nothing dangerous, but you'll feel the current more than usual. Everyone comfortable with that?"

Everyone nodded. Exandra caught Bayard's eye, and he stared back, defiant.

The first challenge was a twenty-foot rappel down a waterfall. The water crashed over rocks, sending up spray that caught the morning sunlight in rainbow patterns.

"Who wants to go first?" Carlos asked.

"I will," Bayard volunteered.

Exandra's hands clenched, but she said nothing.

Carlos checked Bayard's harness and gave him instructions, and then Bayard positioned himself at the edge of the cliff.

For a moment, he just stood there, looking down at the churning water below. Exandra watched as he tested his grip, his hands firm and sure on the thick ropes. His eyes were sparkling in a way they hadn't sparkled for years and Bayard was grinning like a silly fool. As he stood in the mist, with Carlos performing one last check on the gear, the mist from the waterfall formed a halo around his head. Then that halo came alive. Exandra could have sworn she saw arrows shooting at love hearts all around him. He wagged his voluminous brows at her. She noticed his helmet was the exact same bright blue as his hiking shoes. A sticker on the side read "I'm the G.O.A.T."

Exandra couldn't stop herself. "Bayard, please be—"

"Sssh…. I will," he interrupted.

Then, with a wink, he pushed himself backward and jumped over the edge.

Bayard descended smoothly, his movements sure and controlled despite the water streaming over him. At the bottom, he unclipped and looked up at the group and held two thumbs up, triumph written across his face.

Exandra went last, rappelling down with practiced ease. At the bottom, she found Bayard waiting, dripping wet but grinning.

"See?" he said. "I told you I could handle it."

"I do see that now," she admitted.

They waited as the rest of the group descended, and in that moment of relative privacy, Bayard said, "I need to come clean."

"What?"

"The upstream incident. The one that started all this. The Culture Vulture's supposed first incident?" He took a breath. "Zephyr was right. It was me. And I made it all up."

Exandra stared at him. "I know. I mean, *obviously* I knew. What I didn't know was why."

"I guess I hoped that maybe if you caught wind of it, you might change your mind about joining us on the trip. I just..." He laughed in a self-deprecating way. "I just wanted an excuse to stay in touch with you. To have a reason for you to respond."

Exandra was very quiet.

"I'm sorry," Bayard said. "I know it was manipulative and wrong and—"

"I'm using vacation days," Exandra interrupted.

He looked up. "What?"

"For this cruise. I'm not here in an official capacity. I mean, I told them I was planning on doing some investigating, but they didn't think it was serious enough to send an agent, so I used my stockpiled vacation time. I haven't taken a proper vacation in…" She shook her head. "Well, I don't think I've ever taken one. Technically, I could take a few years off with pay at this point."

"You… you're on *vacation*?" Bayard's face was incredulous. He snorted back a laugh.

"And the Gruyère incident," she continued, her voice barely audible. "The temperature disruption, the open doors, the space heater? There was never any real danger to the cheese. That was, in fact, all me. I staged the whole thing."

They stared at each other as the truth settled between them.

"So there really is no Culture Vulture," Bayard said slowly.

"There never was. Just two pathetic old people pretending to be criminals so they could stay near each other."

"We're idiots."

"Complete fools."

And suddenly, impossibly, Exandra started to laugh. Not quite a happy laugh—a slightly hysterical, exhausted laugh. "Oh, gods, the stress we caused poor cheesemakers. We're terrible people! We don't deserve to eat any fondue this Yule."

Bayard found himself laughing, too, the absurdity of it all

hitting him now. "Would it make you feel any better to know I made a generous donation to their charity?"

"Actually, it would," Exandra wiped a tear from her eye. "What kind of charity was it?"

"The Cheesemakers Curse Foundation," Bayard said. "They support artisan cheesemakers who've tragically developed lactose intolerance after years in the trade. Apparently it's an occupational hazard and the flatulence can be debilitating."

"Really?" Exandra pressed her lips together.

"Really." Bayard nodded gravely. "They have to hold their meetings downwind from the nearby villages."

"Oh, my Lords and Ladies... I'm going to be fired for cheese-pionage," Exandra ground.

"Well, if that's the case, we're both going to end up in magical prison."

"Sharing a cell, probably."

"With a bunch of lactose intolerant former cheesemakers."

They laughed until tears ran down their faces, until they had to sit down on a rock because they couldn't stand anymore.

"Okay, my brave goats! Who's ready to continue?" Carlos called out.

They looked at each other, still giggling slightly, and nodded.

BETWEEN A ROQUEFORT AND A HARD PLACE

The next section required climbing over a series of large boulders, working their way upstream through a boulder field where water rushed around, and between the rocks.

Bayard struggled a bit here—his stiff leg made the climbing awkward and more difficult. It was eerily reminiscent of the river and the gorge that he and Exandra had snuck off to when they were still in training to work for The Society.

Twice he had to stop and rest. But he kept going, his jaw set with determination.

Exandra stayed close, ready to help but forcing herself not to offer unless asked.

At one particularly difficult spot, Bayard's cane slipped and he dropped it. He watched helplessly as it clattered down into the water below. For the moment, he was stuck, balanced precariously atop the rock.

"Here," Exandra said, offering her hand.

He took it, and she easily pulled him up to the boulder with her considerable strength.

They sat on top of the boulder together, catching their breath.

"Thank you," Bayard said. He pulled out his wand and summoned the cane back to his side. "Should have used the safety strap. I guess I was a little distracted." He looped the leather strap around his wrist and tightened the safety toggle.

"These things happen. You were doing fine." Exandra waved his thanks away.

"I wasn't, actually. But I appreciate the lie."

They watched the water rushing past, and after a moment, Exandra changed the subject. "So. How about that Brie workshop? The disaster we made…"

"What about it?"

"I couldn't make up my mind because I was so afraid of disappointing you. Of choosing wrong." She took a breath. "I hate the idea of making another mistake, Bay. I don't know if I could take it. Especially after I ruined everything."

"You didn't ruin anything," Bayard said quietly.

"I did. I pushed you to go to that gorge. I pushed you to test your water magic even though you said it was dangerous. I was reckless and stupid and—"

"You didn't force me to do anything," he interrupted. "I was trying to impress you. I wanted you to think I was cool. Brave and capable and worth—" He stopped.

"Worth what?"

"Worth getting to know a little better?" he whispered.

Exandra's breath caught.

"Worth *loving*." He finally got the word out.

"Hey, guys! Let's keep moving," Carlos called from ahead.

They stood, and Bayard was more careful with his cane this time. They didn't talk any more about what he'd just said. They couldn't.

Not just yet.

AFTER AN HOUR of climbing and rappelling, they reached the entrance to the narrow slot canyon.

It was barely wide enough for one person at a time to fit through in some sections. The walls rose fifty feet on either side, and between them, the shallow river rushed by their ankles and knees with surprising force. The recent rains had raised water levels higher than normal, and the current was strong and icy cold.

"This is the challenging part," Carlos said. "We'll walk as a group through the slot now, sometimes wading, sometimes swimming. The water should not be more than waist deep. The current will push against you, but there are handholds carved into the walls. Take your time. Stay close together." He looked at the group. "Anyone want to turn back? No shame in it. The river's a little higher than I'd like."

The other four participants exchanged glances. Two of them decided to head back the way they'd come.

"What about you two?" Carlos asked Bayard and Exandra.

Exandra looked at the churning water, at the narrow canyon walls, and struggled to swallow the fear clawing at her throat. This was too much like that day. Too similar. The water, the rocks, the terrible rushing sound.

"I think we should go back," she said.

"No," Bayard said firmly.

"Bayard, look at it. The current's too strong. This is exactly like—"

"Don't you think I know what it's like?" He shook his head at her. "That's why I need to do it."

"But you could—"

"Fall? Get hurt? Yes. I could." He looked at her. "Or I could make it through. I could prove to myself that one accident ninety years ago doesn't have to control my whole life."

"I can't—" Her voice broke. "I can't watch you get hurt again. I can't be responsible for—"

"You're not responsible for anything that happened then, and you won't be responsible for anything that happens now." He touched her arm gently. "Exandra? There's no going back. Only forward."

"Why?" she demanded. She pulled him aside, dragging him farther down the riverbank. They sat to talk while Carlos assembled the gear for the next stretch of the hike. "Why are we doing this, Bay? Why are we both here on this cruise, pretending to be on a case, and why are you risking hurting yourself again in a gorge? Just tell me why!"

"Why do you think?" Bayard looked deep into her cool blue eyes.

"I haven't the foggiest idea." Exandra wrung her hands.

"Because obviously I still love you, you big, beautiful, purple-haired bruiser!" The words burst out of Bayard and echoed off the canyon walls. He clapped a hand over his mouth, surprised at his own volume. A moment later, he continued, a bit more quietly. "Exandra, I've loved you since we were barely more than kids. I was starstruck when I met you. And I've been your biggest fan for over ninety years. I may not have been out in the field with you, but I've always been there watching, behind the scenes. I've wanted to tell you how I felt a thousand times. But I was always too scared. Afraid you'd pity me or feel guilty or awkward because you don't feel the same way anymore. Or maybe you never did. I kept waiting for the perfect moment to say something. But that moment never happened and when I retired, and I realized I was out of moments, I panicked! I invented the Culture Vulture because I thought it would give me an excuse to keep seeing you."

Exandra stared at him, eyes wide and bright.

"But I'm done waiting for perfect moments and making excuses, Exxie. I think I'm doing this now," he continued, his voice coarse, "because I need to prove it to both of us that I'm not broken. I'm still the man you might have loved if I hadn't—"

"Shut up! I do love you, you fool," Exandra croaked. She waved a hand in front of her face, attempting to shoo away tears as if they were flies. "I've always loved you, Bay. And I couldn't care less if you walk with a limp or if you walk at all. I just can't stand the thought of hurting you. Because if anything else happens to you because of me, I don't know what I'd do."

"You're not going to lose me here, in waist-deep water." Bayard laughed softly. "You heard Carlos's spiel. He's never lost anyone in the gorge. And he's not going to lose anyone today. But I think I do need you to hike through that canyon with me. We both need to do this. Together."

"Are you two coming or not?" Carlos called out to them, diplomatically pretending he hadn't heard their entire confession.

Exandra studied Bayard. His hair was white, and he had a cane gripped tight in one hand. But he was every bit the same man she'd fallen in love with as a young trainee. She trusted him. She knew he knew what he was doing and for the first time in almost a century, she trusted he didn't need her protection so much as her partnership.

"All right," she whispered. "Let's go. I'll be right beside you."

"I wouldn't have it any other way."

THE WATER WAS SHOCKINGLY, teeth chatteringly cold. The kind of cold that took your breath away and made it difficult to speak.

They entered the canyon single file. Carlos went first, then Bayard, then Exandra. The current grasped at them with frozen fingers, trying to trip them up and sweep them all downstream. Bayard gripped the carved handholds in the rock wall with one hand and braced himself with the cane in the other, moving slowly but steadily.

"You're doing great," Carlos called back. "Just keep moving. Don't stop."

The canyon narrowed further. The walls pressed in on either side, and the water rose to their waists, then somewhat unexpectedly, it kept rising to their chests.

"I am sorry!" Carlos called out. "It's higher than I thought. There is no turning back here. We must keep moving."

Bayard held his cane above his head to keep it from being swept away.

Exandra stayed right behind him, one hand always reaching out, ready to catch him if he slipped.

But he didn't slip. He moved with caution and precision, testing each handhold and foothold before fully committing his weight.

They rounded a corner and the current strengthened, surging against them with truly frightening force.

"This is the worst of it. There's a pool ahead," Carlos bellowed, making himself heard above the rushing water. "You must swim for about fifteen feet. The current's strong, but aim for the rock outcropping on the left. You can climb out there."

Bayard nodded, took a breath, and pushed off.

He swam with strong, sure strokes. His leg might be weaker, but his arms were powerful from years of using his cane, and he made it across the pool with only minor course correction.

Exandra followed, her superior strength making it look easy.

They climbed out onto the rock outcropping, dripping and panting.

"One more short section," Carlos said, "and we're through."

They continued on. The walls narrowed even more, barely shoulder-width now. The water churned around their legs. The sound was deafening—rushing water, echoing off stone, filling the world with noise.

And then suddenly, almost unexpectedly, they were through it. The claustrophobic canyon opened up into a much wider area with pools of calm, shallow water, and sunlight streaming down from above.

"We made it," Bayard said, vibrating with relief and triumph. "Exandra, we—"

But Exandra had stopped moving. She stood in the knee-deep water, staring at him with an expression he couldn't read.

"What's wrong?" he asked.

"Nothing's wrong," she said. "Everything's wrong. Bayard, I —" Her voice cracked. "You just walked through a gorge like it was nothing. You're perfectly capable and strong and you didn't need me—" She sobbed. "You didn't need me to protect you. You never needed me at all."

"You're wrong, Exxie. I did need you. I still do. Just maybe not in the way you were thinking."

"I've held onto this guilt for ninety years," she continued. "Sometimes I think it's all I have. This responsibility for what happened to you. This need to keep working, to keep fighting, to somehow make up for what I did to you. And now you're telling me you were actually fine? That I didn't ruin everything?"

"You didn't ruin anything," Bayard said firmly, moving toward her through the water. "If anything, that accident saved me. It gave me permission to stop trying to be something I wasn't. To stop pretending I wanted the same exact things you wanted. To find work I actually loved."

"But—"

"The only thing you ruined," he said, "was any chance I had of finding another partner. Because how could I love anyone else when you were still out there, Exxie? How could I settle for anyone else when I'd spent my whole life only wanting you?"

"Oh, Bay! I don't deserve—"

"Stop it." He moved closer. "Stop telling yourself you don't deserve happiness. Stop punishing yourself for ancient history that wasn't your fault. Stop—"

"How?" she cried. "Tell me how I can just let go of ninety years of guilt and—"

He kissed her.

It wasn't a gentle or tentative kiss. It was fierce and definitive and ninety years overdue. Bayard grabbed the front of her wet jacket in one fist and pulled her to him. Exandra wrapped her arms around him so tightly he could barely breathe, and they made out in the middle of the river like they were teenagers and like they were young adults and like they were trying to make up for every lost year in between then and now. They kissed each other for every missed moment, and for every time they'd been too afraid to reach for each other.

When they finally broke apart, both breathing hard, Bayard pressed his forehead to her chest, delighting in the way it hammered the same beat as his own.

"I love you," he whispered. "I've always loved you. And I don't care how many logistics we have to figure out. I don't care how complicated it is. I'm not letting you walk away from me again."

"I love you, too," Exandra whispered back. "But Bayard, I don't know how to do this. I don't know how we make it work when you're on a cruise ship and I'm—"

"We'll figure it out," he said. "When the time comes, we'll figure it out. But right now, right here, can we just... be?"

She kissed him again, softer this time. "Yes. Yes, we can be."

Ahead of them, in an attempt to give them a bit of privacy, Carlos had suddenly become a geologist. He was enthusiastically lecturing on the many types of rocks that could be observed and identified in the canyon walls, and the effects of erosion. Nobody was paying attention.

Behind them, the river kept churning and rushing, but there was no need to keep fighting the current. They'd made it through. Together.

AGED TO PERFECTION

The following morning, back aboard *The Celestine Queen*, Bayard and Exandra sat together at a corner table in the ship's dining room. Minerva spied them immediately. She could tell something had fundamentally changed between them. So why did everything about their posture and body language still scream uncertainty?

They were sitting much closer than they used to. But they were not touching. They kept glancing at each other and then looking away, mirroring each other awkwardly. When Bayard reached out for the coffee pot, Exandra did the same. Their hands nearly collided, and they both jerked back like they'd been burned.

"Well," Zephyr murmured to Minerva as they collected their breakfast from the buffet, " I'm guessing *something* happened."

"Something..." Minerva agreed. "Though they look more miserable than I'd expect for two people who finally confessed their feelings."

"Don't tell me you're thinking of getting involved again, Minnie," Zephyr warned.

Minerva bit her lip.

"We need to let them work things out on their own."

"I know, I know..." Minerva sighed.

AT THE TABLE beside Bayard and Exandra's, Jasper and Wren presented a stark contrast. They sat pressed up so closely against each other that they practically formed a seal. Jasper's arm was draped around Wren's shoulders. Her hand seemed glued to his knee. They shared a plate of pastries, feeding each other bites and laughing at private jokes. Wren had her camera out, taking selfies together, completely unconcerned with who might see or judge them.

"Would you look at the two of them?" Exandra muttered to Bayard, watching the young couple with envy. "Not a care in the world. No thought about what happens when this cruise ends. No worries about jobs or logistics or—"

"Reality," Bayard finished. "Yes. It must be nice to be so young and optimistic."

"Reckless," Exandra said halfheartedly.

Bayard watched Jasper kiss Wren's temple, watched the way she closed her eyes and melted into him, completely comfortable with their public display of affection. "Maybe," he said. "Or maybe they just know something that we've forgotten in our old age."

Exandra opened her mouth to say something, but Minerva and Zephyr chose that moment to approach.

"Good morning!" Minerva said brightly. "May we join you?"

"Actually—" Exandra started.

"That would be lovely," Bayard said at the same time.

They looked at each other awkwardly.

Minerva and Zephyr sat down anyway, pretending not to notice the tension.

"Did you two enjoy the canyoning activity yesterday?" Zephyr asked innocently.

"It was fine," Exandra said quickly.

"Very educational," Bayard added. "That gorge is a geological marvel."

"Mmm hmmmm." Minerva sipped her tea, her expression carefully neutral. "And did you ever have that talk we suggested?"

Both of them suddenly found their breakfast plates riveting.

"We discussed some things," Bayard said carefully.

"Cleared up a few misunderstandings," Exandra added.

"I see." Minerva exchanged a look with Zephyr. "And are you both feeling... clearer about things now?"

"Crystal clear," Exandra said, her voice tight.

"Absolutely," Bayard agreed, sounding miserable.

Fred, who'd been dozing in his carrier beside Bayard's chair, opened one eye, and quacked skeptically.

"Well," Zephyr said, standing up abruptly and pulling Minerva by the sleeve, "we really should let you two finish breakfast and prep. I can't believe we're already arriving in Italy this morning for the final stop on our tour!"

"The Parma region should be spectacular!" Minerva reluctantly followed Zephyr's lead, pushing back her chair with a scrape. She collected her dishes as he pointed to a free table in the corner, away from the group.

"We'll see you two later," Zephyr said.

After they left, Bayard and Exandra sat in silence for a long moment.

"We really need to talk about what happened," Bayard said.

"I know." Exandra sighed.

"But not here." Bayard used his thumb to wipe some jam off Exandra's chin and she shivered, biting her lip and closing her eyes.

"No. Not here." she agreed. "Maybe... somewhere more private?"

"Great. Shall we go now?"

"Yes," Exandra nodded. "We should go. Immediately."

They stacked their plates quickly, hyperaware of every accidental touch, every loaded glance. When they stood to leave, they moved toward the exit separately, careful to maintain distance.

But at the doorway, Exandra's hand brushed against Bayard's, and the contact sent electricity through both of them.

Their eyes met.

"Storage closet," Exandra whispered in Bayard's ear, sending a thrill straight through him, down to the soles of his feet. "Third deck. Near the library."

Bayard nodded, his heart hammering. "Five minutes."

They heard a plaintive quack from back at the table.

"Ruffled truffles! I almost forgot Fred!" Bayard exclaimed. He smacked his forehead and rushed back for the duck.

THE STORAGE CLOSET was small and cramped, filled with extra linens and cleaning supplies. It smelled of lavender and soap. It was possibly the least romantic location on the entire ship.

None of that mattered the moment the door closed behind them.

Bayard barely had time to set Fred down outside with whispered instructions to "stand guard" before Exandra pulled him into her arms. They kissed desperately, making up for the past hour of sitting together and not touching, and for years of wanting and not having.

"Ye Gods," Exandra breathed against his mouth. "I've been

dying all morning. Sitting there, not being able to touch you, pretending everything was normal—"

"I know," Bayard gasped. His hands found her face, her hair, her shoulders, like he needed to confirm she was real. "Me, too. I kept thinking about yesterday. About the canyon. About—"

She kissed him again, and for several minutes, there was nothing but the raspberry jam and chocolate croissant taste of her, the feel of her strong arms around him and the overwhelming rightness of finally being allowed to hold her as well.

But eventually, reality intruded.

"Bayard," Exandra said, pulling back slightly, her forehead still pressed to his. "We do need to talk about this new development."

"I know."

"Really talk. Not just—" She gestured at the small space. "Not just hide in closets and pretend the rest of the world doesn't exist."

He took her hands in his. "All right. Let's talk."

They stood there, limbs entwined, hands clasped, and suddenly neither of them knew where to start.

"I guess what I need to know is... Is this just a vacation thing?" Exandra asked after some hesitation. "A moment of madness because we're away from our normal lives? Because if that's all it is for you, you have to tell me now. Before I—" Her voice cracked. "Before I fall any further."

"Exxie! You think I could ever see this as just a vacation fling?" Bayard's voice was raw. "I've been in love with you for nearly a century. My entire adult life! Yesterday wasn't a moment of retiree madness. It was ninety years of pressure finally reaching the breaking point."

"Then what happens now?" She pulled her hands free. "You're contracted with the cruise line. This is your dream retirement job. And I'm still with the Society. I have cases, responsibilities, a career—"

"That you hate."

"I don't *hate* it—"

"Don't you?" Bayard challenged gently. "Exandra, I know you've mentioned you're not sure how you might be anything else beside an active duty agent for the Society. That's not the same thing as saying you love what you do."

She tapped her foot, turning slightly away from him. "What else would I do? The Society is my life. It's all I've ever known."

"You could find something new. We could—"

"Could what?" She tilted her head back down to face him. "I quit my job and follow you around on a cruise ship? Become a tag-along spouse, wandering the decks while you work? That's not a partnership, Bayard. That's me giving up my entire identity."

"Or...I could quit, then," he offered. "Come back to land. We could open a—I don't know, a crystal shop or a pet store or—"

"Right. And you'd resent me for the rest of your life for taking away this opportunity you've been so excited about."

"I wouldn't—"

"You would. Eventually. Maybe not tomorrow or next year, but someday you'd look at me and think about what you gave up."

They stared at each other, the impossibility of their situation settling like a weight between them.

"So what are you saying?" Bayard's voice was barely a whisper. "That yesterday was a mistake? That we should just... pretend it didn't happen?"

"I don't know what I'm saying!" Exandra pressed her hands to her face. "I just know that I'm one hundred and eight years old. I've spent my entire adult life building a career with the Society. I've never lived in one place for more than a year. I don't know how to do domestic. I don't know how to just... be still. And you—" She looked at him. "You've built this beautiful new life. Teaching, traveling, sharing your knowledge with people who appreciate it. You're finally doing exactly what you want to do. I can't ask you to give that up."

"You're not asking. I'm offering."

"It's the same thing."

"It's not!" Bayard moved closer, taking her hands again. "Exandra, listen to me. I've spent ninety years being afraid. Yesterday, in that canyon, I stopped being afraid. And I'm not going to start again now just because the logistics are complicated."

"The logistics aren't just complicated, they're impossible."

"Nothing's impossible if we want it badly enough. We are two incredibly smart, resourceful, and determined magical adults. We can do anything!"

"That's naive," she said, half joking but her eyes were filling with real tears now. "Bayard, we're not kids any more. We can't just run away together and make it up as we go. We have responsibilities. Obligations. We're too old to—"

He kissed her again, cutting off her protests.

"We are *not* too old," he said firmly when they broke apart. "Yesterday you watched me climb through a gorge that was eerily similar to the one that nearly killed me ninety years ago. You saw me rappel down waterfalls and navigate slot canyons. Does that seem like someone who's too old for adventure?"

"That's different—"

"Is it? You're the one who's been working dangerous cases for decades. Facing down vampires and dark wizards and who knows what else. And you're telling me you're too old to take a risk on us?"

She laughed through her tears. "When you put it that way—"

"We'll be fine," Bayard said. "I don't know how yet. But we will. Because what's the alternative? Going back to the way things were, pretending yesterday didn't happen, spending another ninety years apart? That's not acceptable. Not anymore."

Outside the closet, Fred quacked urgently.

"Someone's coming," Exandra whispered.

They listened as footsteps approached, paused, and then moved on. Fred quacked again, softer this time, giving them the all clear signal.

"We should go," Bayard said. "We're docking in Italy soon. The tour..."

"Right. The tour." Exandra wiped her eyes. "Bay, I—"

"We don't have to figure everything out today," he said gently. "Let's just take it one step at a time. Okay?"

PRIDE AND PARMESAN

The monastery-turned-creamery sat perched in the rolling hills of the Parma countryside, its ancient stone walls glowing peachy gold in the afternoon sun. It was an architectural treasure, all arched doorways and terra-cotta roofs with a bell tower that still cheerfully chimed out the hours.

"Caseificio San Benedetto," Bayard announced to the group as they disembarked from their shuttle. "Founded by Benedictine monks in 1134, it's one of the oldest continuously operating Parmigiano-Reggiano producers in the world. The monks are not big fans of magic, but they do believe in miracles and they have long believed that the aging process and resulting cheese is akin to a form of blessing. The longer the cheese matured, the more blessings it accumulated."

A robed figure emerged from the main building—an actual monk, elderly and serene, with a kindly wrinkled face and gnarled, calloused hands.

"Welcome, welcome," he greeted them in accented English. "I am Brother Tomasso. We are so honored to host you for your final stop on this remarkable journey."

"Brother Tomasso," Bayard greeted him warmly. "Thank you for accommodating us."

As the group gathered, Minerva noticed several passengers looking around nervously, whispering to each other.

"Do you think this is where the final heist will go down?" someone murmured.

"I don't know. The Culture Vulture has been quiet since Switzerland," another passenger replied.

"Right. So surely they'll strike at the final stop?" the first passenger argued.

"I heard they're only targeting the most precious and rare Yule cheeses," a third person added, raising her eyebrows. She lowered her voice to a near whisper, "and you know how sacred Parmesan is here."

Brother Tomasso looked puzzled. "Strike? Is something wrong?"

Bayard and Exandra exchanged a worried glance.

"Perhaps," Bayard said, "we should address a small matter before we begin the tour."

He moved to the front of the group, Exandra beside him.

"We have an announcement to make," Bayard said. "Over the past two weeks, we've been hearing rumors about incidents occurring at various fromageries. Rumors of sabotage, threats to production. I want you all to know that you don't need to worry. The case has been definitively resolved."

A collective gasp rose from the group. Brother Tomasso held a hand to his chest.

"What does that even mean?" one of the passengers asked.

"The perpetrator has been apprehended," Exandra added, her voice firm and official. "There is no longer any threat to any of the facilities we've visited or to Yule cheese production as a whole."

"Wait. Are you saying you caught the Culture Vulture?" Wren asked, her camera already up.

"The situation has been... handled," Bayard said carefully. "You can all enjoy the rest of the tour without any concerns about sabotage or danger."

But instead of relief, a wave of vague disappointment rippled through the group.

"Oh, okay then..." someone said. "That's—good, I suppose?"

"I was rather hoping for one more final incident," another passenger admitted. "Not that I want anyone to get hurt, of course, but the mystery was exciting."

"Most exciting part of the cruise, honestly," a third person agreed. "I mean, I do love cheese, but there's only so many mold cultures that I can keep straight in my head."

"I'm lactose intolerant and I was still having a blast on this cruise!" announced another passenger.

Minerva watched Bayard and Exandra's faces carefully. They were both clearly gobsmacked by the passengers' reactions, and unsure what to say.

"Well," Brother Tomasso said, diplomatically ignoring the group's disappointment, "perhaps we can still provide you all with some excitement about the magnificence of our sacred Parmesano? Come, let me show you something truly special."

BROTHER TOMASSO LED them through the monastery's original corridors, past thick stone walls that had stood for nine hundred years, and into the monk's aging caves.

They smelled the Parmesan wheels before they saw them. The scent was rich, complex, slightly sweet. Then they rounded the corner and gasped. The stacked shelves stretched three stories up to the vaulted ceiling where fans circulated and the air. It was the most cheese any of them had seen in one place on the entire tour. There had to be at least a thousand wheels of Parmigiano-Reggiano, aging on the wooden shelves. Each one was marked with the official consortium stamp.

"Those wheels are larger than the tires on my motorbike," Wren whispered to Jasper. "I wonder what they weigh?"

"These wheels," Brother Tomasso explained, "weigh approximately eighty-five pounds each. They must age for a minimum of twelve months, but our Yule wheels age for thirty-six months. Three full years of patient waiting, of extra accumulated blessings."

If anyone noticed that the monk refrained from using the word "magic," they did not mention it.

Next Brother Tomasso led them to a special chamber where a single wheel sat on a raised platform, marked with gold leaf and runes.

"This is one of our Yule wheels for the current Yule season," he said reverently. "Made from the milk of our monastery cows, aged for exactly three years to the day, and ready to be broken open tonight for the first time. The first grating of a newly cracked wheel of our special Yule Parmigiano-Reggiano is called 'the angel's snow'. When it is served over the feast on the Yule table, it brings blessings of abundance to all for the coming year."

"How do you know when it's ready?" Jasper asked.

"We know by the date, but we also must listen," Brother Tomasso said simply. He picked up a small silver hammer and tapped the wheel in various places. Each spot produced a different tone. It was a deep, resonant sound. "When the cheese sings in harmony, when all the notes align, we know it has aged to perfection. It is ready."

"So, um... Does that mean we are going to get to try some Parmesan?" One of the passengers asked tentatively. "I'm not sure I recognize that tune."

"The cheese is ready. And the breaking ceremony will happen this evening," Brother Tomasso continued, "but first, we must move this wheel to the preparation room.

Usually we wait for the younger monks, but—" He looked at the massive wheel. "If anyone feels moved to help?"

Exandra stepped forward, arm raised. "I can carry it."

Brother Tomasso looked doubtful. "Signora, it weighs—"

She lifted the wheel as if it weighed nothing, hoisting it onto her shoulder with a grin."Show me the way!"

The group gasped at her show of strength and Brother Tomasso's eyes went wide.

"Or perhaps you do not need help," he said, impressed. "It seems you are rather blessed as well. This way, please, Signora."

As Exandra carried the enormous wheel through the monastery, Bayard watched her with undisguised admiration. This was Exandra fully herself—strong, confident, no longer hiding, attempting to make herself smaller, or holding back.

She caught his eye and smiled back at him.

They saw the copper vats where the cheese was started, watched the salting process, learned about the consortium's strict regulations. It was fascinating, however, that as they completed the tour, all the passengers kept making mildly disappointed comments.

"It's all very interesting, learning about the cheese," one woman said to her companion, "but I keep thinking how much more exciting this monastery would have been with one more mystery to solve. I miss the Culture Vulture."

"I know what you mean," her friend agreed. "The Culture

Vulture added so much sizzle to the journey. Made us all feel like we were part of something big."

"I'd honestly pay extra for a cruise like this with built-in mysteries," a man added. "You know, where we get to play detective. Like a murder mystery dinner, but with cheese."

Bayard and Exandra were walking just ahead of this group. Minerva saw them both stop walking at exactly the same moment.

They turned to stare at each other, and something electric passed between them.

Inspiration.

Excitement.

Hope.

"Are you thinking what I'm thinking?" Bayard asked quietly.

"I think so," Exandra breathed. "Mystery cruises? With fake sabotage? Puzzles to solve? Guests playing detective?"

"You could create the mysteries! Design the scenarios! You know all about conducting investigations."

"And you could still teach the cheese education. Provide the expert knowledge, but toss in an investigatory twist. We'd be perfect—"

"Partners," Bayard finished. "Perfect partners. Working together."

"You wouldn't have to give up the cruise line," Exandra said, the words tumbling out faster now. "I could join you immediately. I wouldn't even have to quit the Society right away. I have enough leave saved up to spend several years away. Oh, Bay! We should pitch this idea to the cruise company this afternoon! Mystery-themed cruises. They're popular with Ordinary folk—why not magical people, too?"

"You'd have to leave the Society eventually."

"I think I'm okay with that," she said, and seemed surprised by her own certainty. "Bay, I'm tired. I'm so tired of fighting and investigating real crimes and seeing the worst of people. But this—" She gestured around them. "Creating mysteries for fun? Giving people adventure without real danger? Working with you every day?" She laughed. "That doesn't sound like giving anything up. That sounds like I'm getting to have everything I want."

"It sounds like winning," Bayard squeezed her hand. Then he lifted it to his lips and kissed it. He didn't care who saw.

They stood in the corridor, other passengers flowing around them, and just stared at each other.

"Are we crazy?" Bayard asked.

"Completely insane, I think." Exandra giggled.

"We'll need to design the whole program from scratch." Bayard tugged thoughtfully at his eyebrow.

"We'll be working together. Every day. All the time," Exandra noted.

"Might drive each other mad." Bayard bit a lip worriedly.

"Almost certainly will." Exandra giggled.

They smiled at each other, and this time when their hands found each other, they didn't let go.

"Let's do it," Bayard said.

"I'm in," Exandra agreed.

FAMOUS LAST CURDS

The atrium of *The Celestine Queen* was all dressed up and decorated for the final Yule feast. Long tables stretched the length of the space, draped in forest green cloth and decorated with evergreen garlands, candles, and small wheels of cheese and flowers serving as centerpieces. The Yule tree at the center glowed with twinkling lights, and the air smelled of fragrant woodsmoke, cinnamon, and the scents of the feast that wafted in from the kitchen.

Everyone had saved their finest clothes for the occasion. There was something about seeing everyone milling about in their finery that made the evening feel extra special.

"This is one for the memory books." Minerva smiled. "I do hope Wren will share some of her photos with us."

She was standing at the entrance, watching and waiting for their special guests to arrive. She couldn't help but feel a deep sense of satisfaction. This cruise, with all its chaos and cheese emergencies and romantic drama, had turned into something special.

"Looks like we'll have quite the turnout," Zephyr said, appearing at her elbow with two glasses of mulled wine. Minerva thought he looked incredibly dashing in his aubergine-hued tuxedo. She'd brought along a long velvet gown in a matching shade. One of her favorites. It was extremely comfortable for formalwear. It even had pockets where she could stash her wand. Such a happy accident that her favorite dress matched his favorite tuxedo. She'd also made herself a crown of flowers to wear, saving one last rose for Zephyr's boutonnière. She pinned it for him now.

"My stars, you look so lovely, my dear." Zephyr spun her around.

"And you're quite fetching as well. Not a single crumb in your beard!" Minerva exclaimed happily.

"We clean up well, don't we?" Zephyr chuckled.

"Oh! Look! They're here! The cheesemakers are arriving." Minerva pointed at the procession making their way up the gangplank.

And there they all were. First came Lukas and Anja from Switzerland, looking slightly overwhelmed by the ship but delighted to be there. Raoul and Geraldo from Spain strode in holding hands and admiring the decorations. When Margot and Claire from France entered the atrium, they were already deep in conversation with Brother Tomasso. He'd explained to them that he'd agreed to delay his return to the monastery just long enough to perform the breaking ceremony.

"Is that Philippe Valmont?" Zephyr asked, surprised to see the French cheesemaker rushing up the gangplank alone. "After the incident at his fromagerie, I'm a little surprised he's joining us again!"

"That's him, all right," Minerva wrinkled her nose.

"Is he bringing his child?" Zephyr asked. The haughty French cheesemaker was wearing a baby carrier against his chest, cradling the bundle close with both arms.

"He's definitely brought his baby, but it's no human child…" Minerva did a double take as Phillipe reached the top of the ramp and she caught a glimpse of the golden rind in the carrier he was clutching. "He brought his family's special Roquefort!" she gasped. "The Yule cheese from his worthiness list. I guess we all made the cut! "

"Now that is what I call character development," Zephyr murmured. "Who would have thought?"

Blythe Meadowsweet was the last to arrive, fashionably late and dancing up the ramp in a whirlwind of ombre silk chiffon and infectious energy. She swept into the atrium like a warm summer breeze, drawing every eye. It was quite the trick, because every time you blinked, her gown seemed to develop a new set of colors. It was like watching the sunset.

"My darlings!" she called out to a crowd of admirers. "What a glorious gathering! I can feel the love in this room—it's absolutely vibrating with all your good energy!"

Philippe, who was reverently setting down his cheese at one of the head tables, looked up at that precise moment and froze.

Their eyes met across the crowded atrium.

"Oh, dear." Minerva elbowed Zephyr in the ribs. "Did you catch that exchange, Zippy? This feast just got a lot more interesting!"

248

FROMAGE THE HEART

Brother Tomasso stood at the center of the atrium, the enormous wheel of thirty-six-month-aged Parmigiano-Reggiano on a round table before him. Beside the wheel sat the traditional tools: almond-shaped knives, the ceremonial hammer, and a small bowl of sanctified salt.

The room fell silent as everyone filed past the wheel to reach their seats at the long tables. A light brush of fingertips, a gentle pat, a moment of connection. One by one, almost instinctively, they reached out to touch it, each one adding their wishes for the year to the wheel.

Bayard and Exandra sat together at the head table. They were not hiding their affection anymore. Their hands were clasped together on top of the table where anyone could see. Fred sat on a plump pillow between them, wearing a tiny pintucked shirt front and bow tie for the occasion.

"My friends," Brother Tomasso began amongst a chorus of clinking champagne flutes as the crowd rallied to call everyone's attention to the start of the ceremony. "My friends," he began again, his voice gentle but carrying through the space, "we gather tonight to celebrate Yule. It is the longest night, but it also represents the return of light, the promise of renewal. And so on this long, dark night, we gather to break open this wheel of cheese, which has aged for three full years in the darkness of our caves, accumulating blessings, waiting for this moment."

He placed his hands on the wheel, and candlelight seemed to gather and reflect off its shimmering golden rind.

"The magic of this ceremony is not in the cheese alone, but in the community. In the gathering of people who have shared an important journey together. Who have faced challenges together. Who have discovered that the best things in life—like the best cheeses—require patience and time."

Minerva saw Wren lean her head onto Jasper's shoulder.

"This cheese began as simple milk," Brother Tomasso continued. "And then, through natural transformation, exposure to ancient cultures, salt of the earth, and the blessings of Father Time, it became something much richer. Just as we, through our experiences and our connections with each other, are constantly being transformed into new versions of ourselves. May we find nourishment, joy, and sustenance from one another as we do from this sacred cheese."

He picked up the ceremonial knife.

"And just as this cheese has reached the perfect moment of maturity, ready to move forward into its next chapter of purpose, so too do we find ourselves at turning points.

Ready to embrace new beginnings. Ready to take what we've learned in our travels and carry it forward into the year to come."

With practiced movements, he inserted the knife into the wheel and began to work it open. The cheese split along its natural fault lines, revealing the pale, sparkling crystalline interior that reminded Minerva of the geodes she used to love opening as a child.

A collective sigh went through the room. The Parmesan was perfection.

"And now—" Brother Tomasso rang a bell. "—we shall partake and share this simple blessing. Together."

He stepped back, and the servers moved forward to begin grating the cheese over the waiting dishes.

"BEFORE WE BEGIN OUR FEAST," Bayard said as he stood, "I'd like to take a moment to thank and share a toast to all of the cheesemakers who have joined us tonight. This cruise has been a journey through the heart of European cheesemaking tradition, and each of you has shared not just your cheese, but your passion, your knowledge, your warmth, and your hospitality."

The passengers burst into a round of applause that went on for quite a while. When the thunderous appreciation died down, Bayard continued with his toast.

He gestured to each cheesemaker in turn. "To Lukas and Anja, who managed to save their Gruyère when a disaster loomed. They were our first hosts. They taught us that you can't rush the process. The best cheese tells you when it's ready. From them we learned that patience and attention are the keys to perfection."

The Swiss couple stood and bowed. Anja was crying happy tears as she thanked them all for hosting them. She jumped up from her seat and stood on a chair, waving her wand toward the four corners of the room, then swirling it in a spiral overhead. With a dramatic singular *whoosh*, the flames beneath all the fondue pots, set at intervals on all the tables, ignited. She curtsied and returned to her seat.

"In Meaux," Bayard announced, "we had the honor of meeting Margot and Claire, from the Maison Du Lait fromagerie, who showed us the art of Brie-making, and who reminded us that partnerships built on love and respect are the most likely to create something beautiful and lasting."

"And that you shouldn't judge a baked Brie by its crust!" Exandra added, blushing when several folk began to clap for her.

The French couple raised their glasses in acknowledgment.

"And then there was Philippe Valmont—" Bayard paused, glass in the air. Everyone could hear the smile in his voice when he went on. "—who taught us that even the most precious traditions are meant to be *shared*. That worthiness isn't about bloodlines or status, but about community and generosity."

Philippe stood, holding up a platter with the wheel of Roquefort he'd brought to the feast. "I have learned," he said stiffly, "that some lessons arrive late in life. But better late than never, non? This Yule cheese was originally meant for my own family. But tonight, I have chosen instead to share it with all of you. Because you have taught me that everyone is worthy of joy and cheese, and I think maybe, we are all family now."

Applause rippled through the room.

"Blythe Meadowsweet," Bayard continued, "who reminded us that life is too short not to embrace color and creativity and a little bit of chaos. That sometimes the most beautiful things come from happy accidents."

Blythe stood and curtseyed dramatically, her scarves billowing. "And happy cows!" she added.

"Raoul and Geraldo," Bayard said, "who shared not just their Queso Luna goat cheese, but their gift of hospitality and wellness. Who showed us that taking time to rest and reflect is just as important as working hard."

The Spanish couple waved, beaming.

"And finally to Brother Tomasso, who has blessed us tonight with both his cheese and his wisdom. Who reminded us that transformation is a gift, and that the best things in life require patience and faith."

The monk bowed his head modestly.

"To all of you," Bayard said as he raised his glass, "thank you for being part of this journey."

"To the cheesemakers!" everyone in the room chorused heartily, cups clinking and champagne overflowing as they took their first of many toasts.

As the first course was served—the Gruyère fondue that had started their journey—the cheesemakers' table came alive with animated discussion.

Lukas demonstrated a dunking technique to Margot, who nodded thoughtfully. Raoul and Geraldo entertained Claire with stories about a recent group of nudists that took over their wellness resort. Their voices rose and fell in musical harmony as they recounted their surprise when they walked into the breakfast hall.

But the most animated discussion was the one happening between Philippe Valmont and Blythe Meadowsweet.

"Your methods are completely unorthodox," Philippe said, his voice carrying across the room. "Tie-dyed cloth? Dream-catchers in the barn? This is not serious cheesemaking!" He tutted and shook his head.

"And your methods are completely stuffy!" Blythe shot back. "All your rules and regulations and golden needles and precious worthiness lists. Where's the joy? Where's the creativity?"

"Cheesemaking is not about joy, it is about *precision*!"

"Everything is about joy!"

The entire atrium had gone quiet, everyone watching the argument unfold like dinner theater.

"Your Roquefort is probably bitter and unimaginative," Blythe declared.

"Your cheddar is probably chaotic and unrefined," Philippe countered.

"How dare you!" Blythe grabbed a cube of her rainbow cheddar and thrust it at him. "I dare you to say that to me again once you've had a taste of this particular nirvana!"

Philippe, affronted, grabbed a piece of his precious Yule Roquefort. "You taste mine first!"

"I accept your challenge." Blythe nodded. "On the count of three. One...Two...Three!"

They both took a bite of the other's cheese from each other's outstretched hands.

Silence.

Philippe's eyes flew open wide. "This is... the flavors are surprisingly complex. The texture is... How on earth did you achieve this crystalline structure?"

"Your Roquefort." Blythe closed her eyes and breathed in deeply through her nose. "Oh, my goddesses! It's magnificent. Those honey notes! They sing! How did you—?"

They stared transfixed at each other.

"What if," Philippe said slowly, "we combined our techniques? Your creative wrapping methods with my traditional aging process?"

"What if," Blythe added, "we created a collaborative cheese? Something that honored both tradition and innovation?"

"It would be revolutionary."

"It would be beautiful."

"We would have to work together. Extensively. Perhaps I should visit Cornwall—"

"Or I should come to France—"

They were standing very close now, both talking faster, their hands gesturing wildly.

"Your passion for cheese—it's intoxicating," Philippe admitted.

"Your knowledge—it's incredibly seductive," Blythe replied.

And then, to the absolute delight of everyone watching, Philippe Valmont and Blythe Meadowsweet flung themselves at each other and shared a kiss that could only be described as French.

The room erupted in applause and cheers and more than a few blushes. Fred, however, hid his head under both wings.

When the two cheesemakers broke apart, both slightly dazed, Philippe said, "We should discuss this collaboration in detail."

"Oh, yes," Blythe agreed, still in his arms. "Very detailed discussions. Possibly over dinner. Many dinners."

"Wait till the dwarves get a load of him!" one of the passengers mumbled, but they still were grinning.

"My money's on the dwarves. Valmont is milquetoast," another passenger said and laughed.

Minerva caught Zephyr's eye and they both started laughing. "Did we just witness another romance beginning?" she asked.

"I think we did," Zephyr replied. "This cruise may be proof that good cheese is even more effective than a love potion."

FINAL CURDS

As the feast progressed through each course—the Roquefort with fresh figs, the Brie baked in phyllo, the rainbow cheddar with accompaniments, the Queso Luna on crostini—the servers prepared for the final course. The Angel's Snow Risotto would be the grand finale of the evening.

Bayard tapped his glass with a spoon in order to call the lively group back to order.

"I'd like to wrap up the evening with a word from a representative from the Celestine Line. She has some exciting cruise news to share with you. She's based in Italy and we are so fortunate to have her here with us tonight. Without further ado, please welcome Eleanor Celestine."

A distinguished-looking witch in a navy silk gown with bright gold buttons rose slowly and proceeded to the podium.

"Before we serve our final course," she announced in perfect English, "I want to thank you all for being part of this Magical Waterways tour. Your enthusiasm and adventurous spirits have made this voyage truly special. All of us at the Celestine Line are grateful that you have trusted us with your travels. We look forward to greeting you again." She smiled warmly at the crowd. "And on that note, I'm pleased to announce that based on the success of this cruise, we'll be expanding our lecture series offerings even further. We have some exciting new programs in development that will combine education with... well, with a little bit more mystery than we originally planned."

Curious whispers rippled through the room as the guests speculated about what this might mean.

"Actually," Eleanor continued, "I'd like to invite Bayard Fontaine and Agent Exandra Thorne to say a few words about these new programs."

Bayard and Exandra looked at each other, and Exandra nodded. Bayard squeezed her hand. They stood up together.

Eleanor handed the microphone back to Bayard and returned to her seat.

"We have an announcement," Bayard began. "Over the past few hours, Exandra and I have been discussing a new collaboration with the cruise line."

"Many of you expressed disappointment," Exandra added, "when we announced that the Culture Vulture had been apprehended. Several of you mentioned that the mystery—the excitement of trying to solve what was happening—was one of your favorite parts of the cruise."

"So we thought," Bayard continued, "what if that experience wasn't a bug, but a feature? What if we created cruises specifically designed around solving mysteries? Nothing dangerous," he added quickly. "Fabricated scenarios, puzzles to solve, clues to find. A chance to play detective while learning about cheese, or wine, or magical history, or any number of subjects."

"Bayard would continue his lecture series, naturally," Exandra said, "and I would design and orchestrate the mysteries. We'd work together to create immersive experiences that combine education with adventure."

"We're calling it Adventures at Sea," they said together. "And the first cruise launches next season."

The room exploded with applause.

"I want to book right now!" someone shouted.

"Can we sign up for the first voyage?" another passenger called out.

Eleanor beamed. "We'll be taking reservations starting next week. I suspect they'll fill up quickly."

Wren, sitting with Jasper, was already jotting notes on her napkin. "This is just incredible," she said. "My article was going to be about a cheese cruise, but now it's about so much more! Love and mystery and transformation and—" She looked at Jasper. "This is the best story I've ever covered."

"Can I be in the article?" Jasper asked hopefully. "With photo credit?"

She kissed him. "Obviously."

After the applause died down and Bayard and Exandra finished answering questions and sat back down, the servers brought out the final course. It was the most perfect risotto any of them had ever seen. The rice was creamy, tender, and expertly cooked. Butter and wine created a rich, savory, melt-in-your-mouth base. But it was not ready to be consumed. Not just yet.

Brother Tomasso stood. "Now," he said, "we add the Angel's Snow."

The servers moved through the room with the freshly grated Parmigiano-Reggiano. And as they sprinkled it over each dish, something quite remarkable happened.

The cheese didn't merely fall onto the risotto. It floated.

Tiny flakes of golden-white Parmesan drifted and fluttered like snow, each piece catching the candlelight and casting rainbow prisms about the room as it made its way down to the dish.

And as the Angel's Snow settled into the risotto, everything in the atrium seemed to shimmer. Colors became brighter, richer. The aromas intensified. Suddenly everyone could smell not just the cheese, but every herb, every note of butter, every complex flavor layered in the dish.

"The blessing of abundance," Brother Tomasso said softly. "What was already good becomes magnificent. What was already beautiful becomes radiant. The snow doesn't change the dish. It reveals what was always there, waiting to be appreciated."

Outside the windows, as if responding to the magic inside, real snow began to fall. Soft, fat flakes drifting down from the dark sky, settling on the ship's deck, on the distant mountains, transforming the world into something new.

263

A FONDUE FAREWELL

After the feast, as guests mingled and the evening mellowed into something softer and more intimate, small groups gathered in quiet conversation.

Jasper found Wren on the deck, watching the snow fall. He had something small in his pocket—the snow globe he'd bought at the holiday market, which felt like a lifetime ago.

"Wren," he said. "I have something for you."

She turned, curious. "Oh?"

He pulled out the small wrapped box. "It's nothing much. Just something I saw and thought of you."

She unwrapped it carefully, and when she saw the delicate glass sphere with the tiny camera painted inside, surrounded by stars, her eyes welled up.

"Jasper, it's beautiful."

"It's about capturing memories," he said. "The light we

save from moments that might otherwise fade. Like this cruise. Like—" He took a breath. "Like us."

"About that," Wren said. "I know you're going back to London to finish your degree, and I'll be traveling for work, and we haven't talked about—"

"I'll be in London for the next eighteen months," Jasper said. "And you said you're covering the opening of that new hotel in a few weeks?"

"The Enchanted Mayfair," Wren confirmed. "Three-week assignment."

"So we'll see each other then," Jasper said. "And after that —well, we'll play it by ear. Where there's a will, there's a way. Right?"

She kissed him, soft and sweet and full of promise. "Right."

ON THE OPPOSITE side of the ship, Bayard and Exandra stood at the railing, also watching the snow fall on the dark water. They stood close, Bayard's arm around Exandra's waist, her head resting atop his.

"I can't believe this is real," Exandra said in hushed tones. "I keep thinking I'll wake up and it will have all been a dream."

"If it is," Bayard replied, "then we're both having the same dream. And I'm okay with that."

"Adventures at Sea," she said, testing the title. "Our partnership. Working together every day."

"Terrifying, isn't it?"

"Absolutely." She smiled. "I can't wait."

They stood in comfortable silence, watching the snow transform the city into something shiny and new. Inside, through the steamy windows, they could see the warm glow of the party continuing—friends and food and celebration.

"Thank you," Exandra said.

"For what?"

"For not giving up on us. For being brave enough to face your fears in that canyon. For ninety years of patience and love, even when I was too blind to see it."

"Thank you," Bayard countered, "for being strong enough to let go of guilt. For taking a chance on something new. For loving me despite everything."

"Not despite everything," Exandra corrected. "Because of everything."

Their lips pressed together, soft and sure, as the snow fell around them.

INSIDE, Minerva and Zephyr stood near the Yule tree, watching the various conversations around them.

"We should make this a tradition," Zephyr said. "Yule cruises. Something to look forward to every year."

"I'd like that," Minerva agreed. "Though hopefully with less sabotage and deception."

"I don't know," Zephyr said, grinning. "Worked out pretty well this time."

"Except we completely forgot about the cheese forks." Minerva sighed.

"That's because you were far more focused on a different hobby." Zephyr's eyes twinkled.

They watched as Bayard and Exandra slipped away toward the deck, seeking a moment alone. Brother Tomasso was having an animated discussion with the other cheesemakers about collaboration and innovation. Philippe and Blythe were tucked in a corner, completely absorbed in each other. And Jasper and Wren danced slowly near the windows.

"We did good work, though," Minerva said.

"We did," Zephyr agreed. "Though I think they did most of it themselves, in the end."

"They just needed a push."

"Several pushes."

"And a fake escape room."

"And a canyon."

They both laughed.

"I'm looking forward to going home," Minerva said. "To Primrose Court and the Squeaky Wheel. To our fromagerie and our community. I can't wait to share all these cheeses and traditions with everyone."

"And to tell everyone the story of how two more stubborn people finally found their way back to each other," Zephyr added.

"That, too."

Suddenly, Fred waddled up to where Minerva and Zephyr stood together. He looked up at them, tilted his head, and quacked once—a sound of profound vindication.

"You're so right, Fred," Minerva said, reaching down to scratch his head. "And it all worked out in the end."

The duck quacked again, agreeing, before waddling off to shadow someone who might drop cracker crumbs.

Zephyr pulled Minerva close, and they danced slowly in the warm glow of the Yule tree, surrounded by good food, good friends, and the magic of the season.

WHEN THE PARTY ended and the last passenger was tucked into bed, *The Celestine Queen* sailed on through the snowy night, carrying its cargo of happy couples and good cheese and new beginnings. Above, the stars shone bright. Below, the water reflected the lights of the ship like scattered diamonds.

And somewhere in the night, carrying on the wind, you could hear the distant sound of a call duck's satisfied quack.

The End

IF YOU HAVE ENJOYED READING this novel, I hope you will take a moment to rate and/or review it! Your ratings help others find their way to the world of Primrose Court.

Please check out the Natural Magic Series to learn more about the characters from this story. You won't want to miss how Minerva and Zephyr got back together!

If you'd like bonus scenes, book recs, updates, and a peek inside my crazy writing life, please visit my linktree where you can sign up for my mailing list and catch up with me on all the socials.

THE CHEESEBOARD OF CONTRIBUTORS

This book could never have happened if not for all the laissez faire babysitters who let me stay up watching reruns of The Love Boat and Fantasy Island in the 80s, even though I was supposed to be in bed. It was a lot of Aaron Spelling at an impressionable age and this book is the glorious result.

I probably snacked on cheese while I watched. Let's just say that I did. And let's pretend I'm not lactose intolerant while we're at it.

Some cheeses are worth suffering for!

To my dear husband, who's always up for a sunset charcuterie and who laughs at my worst puns, and who forgave me for writing the entire time we were on our cruise... You are my Zippy!

To my friends who insisted that the world needs more levity right now and I might still be taken seriously after writing this snack of a book. We'll see about that.

To my awesome, accurate and speedy editor Sara, my undying gratitude. Without you this book would just be toast.

I also cannot write a book about cheese without mentioning my dear friend and partner in cheese crimes, Julia Beck.

www.ingramcontent.com/pod-product-compliance
Lightning Source LLC
Chambersburg PA
CBHW061232310726
48971CB00007B/2036